'She's moonlight and magic,

frost and glitter,

stars and darkness,

mischief in a teacup.'

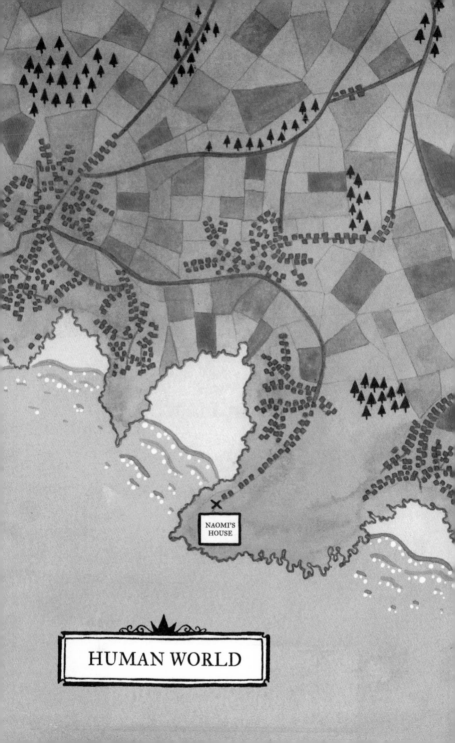

NAOMI'S
HOUSE

HUMAN WORLD

ENTRANCE
AND EXIT TO
WISKLING
WOOD

STREAM

TISKA'S
HIDEOUT

For Victoria Stitch,

who would be furious if this book
was dedicated to anyone else.

OXFORD
UNIVERSITY PRESS

Great Clarendon Street, Oxford OX2 6DP
Oxford University Press is a department of the University of Oxford.
It furthers the University's objective of excellence in research, scholarship,
and education by publishing worldwide. Oxford is a registered trade mark
of Oxford University Press in the UK and in certain other countries

Copyright © Harriet Muncaster 2022

The moral rights of the author have been asserted

Database right Oxford University Press (maker)

First published in 2022

British Library Cataloguing in Publication Data

Data available

ISBN: 978-0-19-277358-6

1 3 5 7 9 10 8 6 4 2

Printed in India by Manipal Technologies Limited

Paper used in the production of this book is a natural,
recyclable product made from wood grown in sustainable forests.
The manufacturing process conforms to the environmental
regulations of the country of origin.

HARRIET MUNCASTER

VICTORIA STITCH
FREE AND
FAMOUS

OXFORD
UNIVERSITY PRESS

CHAPTER I

THE HUMAN WORLD . . .

VICTORIA Stitch huddled up against the cave wall and wrapped her velvet cape tightly around her. With a shivery, icy hand she took out her wand, *Celestine's wand,* and waved it so that a shower of diamond sparks rained down onto the little pile of seaweed in front of her. Immediately, it burst into a crackling fire. Victoria Stitch stuck out her hands and warmed them, the cherry-pink flames flickering up onto her pale face in the gloom. Despite the cold and the fact that she had no place to go, Victoria Stitch was still feeling euphoric after her escape from Wiskling Wood earlier that morning. It had been easy to get past the guards at the exit. They hadn't been expecting to come up against a wiskling like her. A wiskling who

1

knew forbidden magic. She'd used the sleeping spell on them and then slipped through the gate. Easy.

Victoria Stitch smiled smugly as she stroked Stardust, her little draglet, in the light of the fire. Stealing Celestine's wand and bloom, and using a remembered spell from the book of forbidden magic, the *Book of Wiskling,* had been a bad thing to do, but she didn't care. She hated Wiskling Wood and all the wisklings in it—apart from Celestine, of course. She'd had no choice but to leave. She didn't belong there. She didn't belong anywhere. She was better off alone. Out here she was free! The wiskling authorities would never be able to find her in the human world. It was too big. She could do what she liked, as long as she made sure she was never spotted by a human. The world was *hers*.

She opened her black-velvet backpack and took out a flask of her special dark, hot chocolate, and some biscuits, which she shared with Stardust. Together they munched them in front of the fire, listening to the crackles and the drip-drip of water coming off the seaweed slimed walls of the cave. This had been a good place to hide. For now. But Victoria Stitch knew she would have to find somewhere else to settle soon. She couldn't stay in a dark, damp cave forever. Outside, the wind whirled, the snow swirled and the sea roared and crashed against the rocks. Victoria Stitch had never seen the sea before, and earlier she had sat on a pebble on the beach, staring at it, marvelling at the way the waves rolled right in towards her and then back out again.

And then she had seen them: the humans. Victoria Stitch had never seen humans before, though she had read about them in books. Here they came, appearing over the horizon, two giants plodding their way down to the sea. Victoria Stitch sat on her pebble, frozen to the spot. She wasn't afraid of being seen—she was so tiny compared to them. It was just a shock to realize *how* tiny. Was she really so *insignificant*?

No. She was a *princess* she reminded herself. And if it hadn't been for the stupid wiskling authorities, and Lord Astrophel, she would have been *Queen*— and she and her twin, Celestine, could have ruled together.

Victoria Stitch had adjusted her crown. Then she got up off the pebble, hopped onto her bloom, and retreated to the cave.

Later, after it had stopped snowing, Victoria Stitch left the cave and flew up into the icy air on her bloom, *Celestine's bloom*. She wanted to explore. It was dusk, and the snowy beach and cliffs shone bright white in the light of the rising moon. No one would spot her at this time of evening. She flew fast up the beach, whizzing towards the cluster of box-like houses that huddled on top of the cliffs. Golden-yellow squares shone out from each house, and for the first time,

Victoria Stitch felt a pang of loneliness, out here all alone in the cold, in a place she didn't know. For the first time since leaving the wood, she let thoughts of Celestine creep into her head and her heart immediately ached.

Celestine.

Things would never be the same again. Her sister, her *twin*, was Queen of Wiskling Wood now. She had duties. The days when it was just the two of them, against the world, were long gone. Victoria Stitch blinked, refusing to let any tears fall. They would probably just freeze to ice on her face anyway.

But now other thoughts threatened to come spilling into her head too. Before Celestine, there was another queen—Queen Cassiopeia. Victoria Stitch remembered with a lurch, being accused of her murder and thrown into prison. Even after Celestine had helped to clear her name, Victoria Stitch had still had her wand and bloom confiscated permanently. It had been too late for redemption by then. She had a *reputation*. Celestine had been put on the throne instead of her. There was no one else left in line. No other babies born of the precious, diamond crystal. And Celestine, born of an impure diamond along with her twin, would have to do.

Victoria Stitch sniffed and shoved the memories

away. She looked around and realized that she was flying towards a human cottage. She landed carefully on the window sill and peered inside, pressing her hands against the cold glass. It looked so light and bright inside. Victoria Stitch guessed this room must be a kitchen because there was a countertop with a sink in it, a shelf full of stripy crockery, and a stove with a pot of something bubbling on it. She couldn't believe how giant everything was! Victoria Stitch felt her stomach rumble. She had eaten all the biscuits from earlier. She could, of course, magic up some food (she still remembered *that* forbidden spell from the *Book of Wiskling*) but where would she eat it? Out here in the cold, freezing to death? No, she needed to get inside a human house somehow, without being seen, and then she could hide. She needed warmth.

Victoria Stitch got back onto her bloom and began to make her way carefully round the walls of the house, looking for an opening. Her heart pitter-pattered in her chest. Was this what a wiskling explorer would do? She knew it was probably not. Explorers usually trained for a year or more to learn how to navigate the human world safely and stay hidden. They had to earn a badge before being allowed to leave Wiskling Wood. And there were lots of rules they were supposed to stick to. Victoria Stitch knew none of these rules, except the most important one: *never be seen*. She stopped in the air, holding on tightly to her bloom as it was buffeted this way and that in the wind, wondering if she really dared to try and enter a human dwelling. It would be an incredibly risky thing to do. Humans could be dangerous. All wisklings were taught that from a young age. But the warmth and light were so tempting. And Victoria Stitch was feeling reckless . . .

She was in front of a door with a letterbox in it. A letterbox! It would be the perfect size for her to slip through. She made her way towards it and pushed against the metal flap, sticking one leg through and then the other and finally her whole body, hoping that there was nobody on the other side; there was no way of telling. The letterbox snapped shut behind her with a clatter and Victoria Stitch was through, hovering in the air on her bloom in the hallway.

Standing right in front of her was a human.

CHAPTER 2

FOUR MONTHS LATER—WISKLING WOOD . . .

CELESTINE was in her study in the Royal Oak Palace, frowning over a long and boring letter that Lord Astrophel had sent her to look over. He was always sending her things to 'look over', though she wasn't sure why he bothered. He never took her opinion or her advice on anything.

Celestine had thought, being Queen, that she would be the one to make the final decisions, to have the final say. But somehow Lord Astrophel, her chief advisor, always managed to overrule her. It felt as though he was pulling invisible strings in the background, controlling everything that happened in

8

the wood with something that she did not have access to. Celestine didn't know how he did it!

And she didn't like it.

It made her feel uncomfortable, as though she was just a thing for show. A bit of glamour at the front, while Lord Astrophel manipulated everything from behind. She had tried to bring it up with him a few times, but he always shut her down with such a dangerous, warning look in his eyes that she didn't dare to go further. It felt much harder to stand up to him now that Victoria Stitch was no longer in Wiskling Wood.

Suddenly there was a light *tap tap* on the door.

'Come in,' said Celestine, putting down her ink pen. A wiskling with a puff of peach-coloured hair piled up on top of her head walked into the room. It was her maid—Minoux.

'Good morning, Minoux!' smiled Celestine, relieved at the interruption. 'How are you?'

'I'm well, thank you, Your Majesty,' said Minoux, and smoothed down her crisp, white frilly apron. Celestine winced slightly. She had never quite got used to being called 'Your Majesty.' She had told Minoux to stop countless times—they were friends now, after all. But Minoux didn't seem to be able to shake old habits.

'Tiska's here to see you,' said Minoux.

'Oh!' said Celestine, jumping up from her chair immediately, her heart racing with excitement and trepidation. Tiska!

Together, Celestine and Minoux hurried down the palace's grand, crystal staircase. Celestine's antennae fizzed with golden sparks. Could it be that Tiska and Ruby had *actually*, *impossibly*, managed to find Victoria Stitch? Or was Tiska just here to give her an update? Yes that's probably what it was . . . but . . . she couldn't help feeling hopeful. It had been four months and her heart still ached for her twin with an awful emptiness. She doubted anyone else in the wood felt the same way she did. A lot of wisklings had been glad when Victoria Stitch had disappeared after all the trouble she had caused, although there were a lot who felt uncomfortable about it too. Who knew what she could be up to, now that she was no longer safe within the confines of the palace?

Celestine and Minoux rounded the corner of the grand staircase. There was the entrance hall with its gigantic tinkling rose and moonstone chandelier and crystal tiled floor and . . . standing next to a guard in front of the great front doors was TISKA!

Celestine almost tripped down the last few steps in her hurry to reach her old friend. She flung herself

on Tiska, holding onto her wiry body, her eyelashes tangling in Tiska's wild green hair. It had been three months since they had seen each other.

'It's so good to see you!' said Celestine, as she dragged Tiska away from the guard and outside to the palace gardens where they could speak in private. They sat down on a patch of mossy grass beneath a clump of crocuses, their lilac petals glowing in the spring morning sunshine.

'And you!' said Tiska. 'I've missed you so much! But listen, I've got something really important to tell you! I came back to Wiskling Wood to tell you as soon as I found out about it! The news will be all over the wood soon!'

'What?!' Celestine felt her antennae explode with glittery anxious sparks. 'Have you found Victoria Stitch? *How* could you have found her!? Where is she?'

Tiska looked grave.

'Victoria Stitch is famous,' she said.

Chapter 3

Four months earlier—the human world . . .

Victoria Stitch felt frozen to the spot, hovering in the air on her bloom.

She'd been seen.

She'd been *seen!*

She should have been more careful coming through the letterbox! She should have waited until all the lights were off and the human had gone to bed! Suddenly she seemed to regain control of her body and she shot up towards the ceiling on her bloom, out of the human's reach. The human gazed upwards, mouth open, eyes wide like saucers.

'Wait! Don't go!' it said.

Victoria Stitch stared down into the human's face. Her heart was beating like a wild thing. The human had made it sound like she was free to leave if she wanted to, and that made her feel less afraid.

'Please stay!' said the human. 'I've never seen a real fairy before!'

Victoria Stitch blinked and opened her mouth to retort that she wasn't a fairy—whatever *that* was. But then she shut it again. Maybe it would be better if the human *did* think she was a fairy. It would be much safer than revealing anything at all about wisklings.

'I'm a fairy *queen*.' The words fell out of her mouth before she could stop them. But it was half-true wasn't it? She was royal, after all. A princess.

'Ohh!' said the human in breathless wonder. 'Is that why you're wearing a crown? It's so tiny! I'm Naomi.' She held out her hand and then took it back laughing.

'Well, that's not going to work, is it!'

Victoria Stitch raised an arched eyebrow. She didn't trust anyone except Celestine. And humans could be dangerous. All wisklings knew that. They were so big. Unpredictable. They had the power to crush a wiskling with one squeeze of the fist. It wasn't safe to be under their power. She needed to be *really* careful. She stayed where she was, high up above the human's head, hovering out of reach.

'I won't hurt you!' said Naomi, putting her hands behind her back. 'I promise! This is just amazing! Just incredible . . . I can't believe fairies actually exist!'

'Well, they do!' said Victoria Stitch, starting to feel a little bit braver. 'And I am the *Queen* of all of them! I was just having a . . . holiday in the human world and came across your house. Is that soup I see bubbling away in the kitchen?'

'Yes!' said Naomi, breathlessly. 'Do you want some?'

'I suppose I may as well, while I'm here,' said Victoria Stitch haughtily, but she still didn't come down from the ceiling.

'Of course,' said Naomi. 'Your Majesty. Is that what I'm supposed to call you?'

'*Yes!*' said Victoria Stitch, and the word came out of her much more fiercely than she had meant it to. All the hurt and rejection of everything that had happened in Wiskling Wood came flooding back again. It all still felt so raw. She had been scorned by everyone and forced to live inside the confines of the palace grounds while she watched her sister become the one thing she had always wanted to be—Queen. But, here . . . here was a human, who seemed happy to believe she was a queen—she could pretend to be a fairy for a while if this human was prepared to treat

15

her with the respect she so deserved.

'Do you live by yourself?' asked Victoria Stitch, as she followed Naomi into the kitchen, still making sure to keep well out of reach.

'No,' said Noami. 'I live with my mum. I'm only thirteen! She's out at the moment, though—but she's working, so don't worry.'

'Oh,' said Victoria Stitch. She hadn't realized the human was a young one. She was wearing a black top and tights, a red tartan skirt with frills round the bottom, and a pair of big, fluffy socks. She had lots of jewellery on, too, and it tinkled as she walked.

'Here, let me open a window a crack,' said Naomi. 'You'll feel safer if you know you're able to leave any time you like. But I promise I won't harm you.'

Victoria Stitch landed on the window sill next to the open window, shuddering as the icy breeze whirled round her legs.

Naomi stepped back a few paces, still staring, mesmerized, and Victoria Stitch noticed that her hair had been pinned back with glittery red heart clips.

'I didn't know fairies flew around on flowers!' she said. 'I thought they had wings!'

'Oh,' said Victoria Stitch, 'well . . .' She wasn't *actually* sure exactly what a fairy was, but it seemed like Naomi hadn't even believed they existed before

now, so maybe it didn't matter. She could make something up.

'Humans *think* we have wings,' said Victoria Stitch. 'But actually, we don't.'

Naomi stepped forward, peering closer and Victoria Stitch took a step back.

'Sorry!' said Naomi. 'I just can't take my eyes off you! Your little antennae, they keep sparking! And your ears! So pointed and lovely. And those eyelashes! They're as long as whiskers!'

Victoria Stitch felt the corner of her mouth twitch into a smile. She enjoyed being admired. She had had no idea that humans could be so friendly.

'Sorry!' said Naomi. 'I know it's rude to stare.'

'It's alright,' said Victoria Stitch rather beginning to enjoy herself. 'I don't mind if you stare.' She stuck out her leg and pointed it, fluttering her long, long wiskling eyelashes. She was feeling braver and braver all the time. A daring recklessness was growing inside her. A defiance. Here she was talking to a human! The thing all wisklings are forbidden from ever doing. She could feel her badness creeping in again . . . and she liked it!

Naomi hurried over to the stove and took the pan off the heat. She rummaged around in a drawer and took something out.

'A thimble!' she said triumphantly. 'I know it's not a proper bowl and you are a queen but . . .'

'It will do,' said Victoria Stitch, graciously. She sat down on the windowsill with her legs hanging over the edge, swinging them back and forth. Naomi washed the thimble and then filled it with some soup, bringing it over to Victoria Stitch and putting it gently down beside her. Victoria Stitch didn't even flinch. She was surprised at how comfortable she already felt with Naomi. She never usually liked or trusted anyone.

Except Celestine, of course.

Naomi sat down at the giant table and put her own bowl of soup in front of her. But she didn't eat it. She was still too busy gazing at Victoria Stitch.

'Will you tell me a bit about where you come from?' she asked. 'Do you live in Fairyland? Do you have magic there?'

'Oh yes!' said Victoria Stitch, carelessly, sipping delicately at her soup in the rather unwieldy thimble. 'We have magic, but we're not allowed to use any of the really good spells. Wisklings just use magic for boring stuff. Turning lights on and off, that kind of thing. All the good spells are in a forbidden book. *No one's* allowed to own a copy of it anymore.'

'Wisklings?' said Naomi.

Victoria Stitch coloured. She hadn't meant to let that slip out.

'You can't tell anyone I'm a wiskling!' she said, jumping up in a panic. 'You have to swear! Swear now!'

Naomi held up both her hands.

'I swear!' she said. 'You can trust me. I promise. I've never even heard of wisklings before!' And somehow Victoria Stitch sensed that Naomi was telling the truth. She sat back down, feeling a strange mixture of elation, guilt, and pride. She had just committed one of the worst crimes a wiskling could ever commit. She had told a human about their hidden world. The badness was growing bigger and bigger, threatening to engulf her.

'So, tell me about the forbidden book,' said Naomi. 'What kind of spells are in it? Why aren't . . . *wisklings* allowed to know them?'

'Because the spells are dangerous,' explained Victoria Stitch. 'Spells to make you invisible, spells that can magic things up from thin air, spells that can kill with one point of a wand!'

'You have a real wand?' gasped Naomi.

Victoria Stitch nodded, producing Celestine's beautiful wiskling wand from inside her cape. The star at the top of it was made from a diamond—hers

20

and Celestine's birth crystal.

'Wisklings can only do magic with their own birth crystal,' said Victoria Stitch. 'It's used to make our wands and it can be powdered down to be put in potions! That's how my bloom flies, too, you know. There's a shard of my birth crystal inside the stalk.'

'Your wand is so tiny and sparkling,' whispered Naomi, gazing down at Victoria Stitch in awe. 'Does it really do real magic?'

'Yes,' boasted Victoria Stitch, a mischievous expression passing across her face. 'And unlike other wisklings, *I've* done all sorts of exciting wand-and-potion magic! *I* had a copy of the *Book of Wiskling*— don't ask me how, I just did—and I remember quite a few forbidden spells from the book.'

Naomi stared at Victoria Stitch, a flicker of fear in her eyes. 'How come you had a copy of the *Book of Wiskling*?' she asked. 'Is it because you're the Queen?'

'I . . .' Victoria Stitch faltered. Suddenly she felt a strange compulsion to open up to Naomi.

'I *should* have been Queen,' she said, after a moment. 'But the title was taken away from me. My twin sister and I, we were born from a diamond, and I was born first. All wisklings are born from crystals, but a diamond means you're royal. They don't come along very often. Our diamond had a black mark in

21

it—*a Stitch*—so it was declared impure, and my sister and I were relegated to live ordinary, wiskling lives instead of being sent to live in the palace.'

She scowled at the memory.

'But that's a bit unfair!' said Naomi. 'Why should it have mattered if your diamond had a black mark in it?'

'Exactly!' cried Victoria Stitch, passionately. 'But Lord Astrophel—the head of the wiskling authorities—decided it was impure, and that was that.'

'How awful!' said Naomi.

'It was!' agreed Victoria Stitch, pleased that Naomi could see her point of view. 'So, I decided to do something about it. I met someone, someone who I *thought* was a friend, who said they could help me. She had a forbidden copy of the *Book of Wiskling* and we learned magic from it. I used it to try and get to the throne.'

'Ooh!' said Naomi, her eyes sparkling with excitement. 'What sort of magic?'

'Oh, nothing *that* bad,' lied Victoria Stitch. She decided to skip over the details. How she had used a deception spell to get hundreds of wisklings to sign a petition, demanding she be crowned Queen of Wiskling Wood. How she had used illegal, magicked money to build herself a huge expensive palace, which the authorities had ransacked and found the *Book of Wiskling* inside. How she had been accused of murdering poor Queen Cassiopeia, and how her perfect sister Celestine had eventually been crowned Queen instead of her.

'I was treated *very* unfairly,' she said. 'Anyway, I won't go into it, but some *things* happened . . . And now my sister Celestine is Queen of Wiskling Wood!'

'Oh!' said Naomi. 'You must hate your sister for taking the throne!'

'No,' whispered Victoria Stitch. Suddenly she felt an intense stab of guilt for telling Naomi about Wiskling Wood. What if Naomi didn't keep her promise to not tell anyone about wisklings? What if humans all started *looking* for wisklings? Humans couldn't be trusted! It would put all wiskling explorers in much more danger. But it was too late now. She'd already done it. And now she couldn't stop the words from spilling out.

'Why did you leave?' asked Naomi.

Victoria Stitch shrugged.

'I don't belong,' she said simply.

Naomi nodded, pausing a moment to have a spoonful of soup.

'Can you tell me where Wiskling Wood is?' she

asked. 'I'd love to see it!'

Victoria Stitch shook her head vehemently.

'I can *never* tell you that,' she said. 'And even if I did tell you where it was, you wouldn't be able to see it. It's surrounded by a ring of magic to keep it hidden. Only wisklings can see it and go in and out.'

'Do wisklings often come into the human world, then?' asked Naomi.

'Explorers do,' said Victoria Stitch. 'Mostly to get supplies—ingredients and things that don't grow in Wiskling Wood, like chocolate!' Her eyes sparkled. 'Some explorers just come to the human world for the adventure, though. But they are never, *never* supposed to be seen. Wisklings absolutely cannot risk being at the mercy of humans. You must promise to never ever tell anyone about me! Even your mum!'

'I won't!' said Naomi earnestly. 'I promise ... Your Majesty.'

Victoria Stitch smiled again. She hadn't felt like this in a long time: properly *seen*, admired, noticed.

There was silence for a few moments in the kitchen, and Victoria Stitch took the opportunity to look around more closely. On the walls of the kitchen, there were lots of pictures made from shells and frosted sea glass arranged into beautiful, gradated patterns. More shells and sea glass had been bottled up into jars and put on the kitchen shelves.

'Did you make those?' asked Victoria Stitch, gesturing to the pictures. She wasn't particularly interested in them, but it felt like time to deflect the attention away from herself for a while. Before she got carried away and said something she regretted.

'No,' said Naomi. 'They're my mum's. They're beautiful, aren't they? She's a really good artist. She never has time for her art anymore, though.'

'Why not?' asked Victoria Stitch.

'She's always working to pay the bills,' said Naomi. 'I know she hates her job, though. But she never earned enough money from her art. That's why she's so against me going to art school.'

'Art school?' said Victoria Stitch.

'Yes!' said Naomi, her face brightening at the thought. 'I want to study fashion! Mum says it's a waste of time, though. She thinks I need to focus on my other lessons at school more. Or I'll end up like her.' Naomi's face fell again and she swirled her spoon round her soup bowl. 'I don't think she really understands how important it is to me.'

'I understand,' said Victoria Stitch.

'You do?' said Naomi.

'Yes,' said Victoria, and was surprised to feel tears prickle at her eyes. She wiped them away angrily.

She knew *exactly* how it felt to be so passionate about something but have nobody believe in her. 'Maybe I could help you make money for your mum somehow,' she said. 'If money isn't a problem, then maybe she'll think differently about art school. I have a magic wand. I remember the duplication spell from the *Book of Wiskling*. I could duplicate some money for you . . .'

Naomi stared.

'That would be fraud!' she said, shocked.

Victoria Stitch shrugged.

'It *is* tempting,' said Naomi, her eyes beginning to glitter. 'My mum has to work so much! She has two jobs just to pay the mortgage on this house and she's hardly ever here. I'm always alone . . . But, no. I can't. It would just get Mum into trouble if anyone found out. She's already stressed enough as it is. The hours at one of her jobs have been cut lately and now we almost can't afford this house at all! Mum keeps talking about moving to a flat. But still . . . using *magic* to make money . . . it would be a criminal thing to do . . .'

Victoria Stitch blushed. She had done much worse back in Wiskling Wood.

'But you mustn't lose your house!' she said emphatically. She knew exactly how *that* felt too! The wiskling authorities had torn down her beautiful gothic palace, with all its turrets and sparkling chandeliers.

Naomi looked down sadly at her soup.

'There's not much *I* can do about it. Mum's finding it hard to make ends meet since . . . Dad died. Anyway . . .' She looked up, fixing a bright smile back onto her face. 'Never mind all that. I want to talk about you. Will you stay a little longer? I'd love it if you did! It gets lonely here in the evenings when Mum's out.'

Victoria Stitch blinked, surprised and slightly irked by the swelling of affection she was starting to feel for this human. They had more in common than she could ever have thought possible. She didn't have a father either. Or a mother, for that matter. She had nobody but Celestine.

'I suppose I *could* stay the night,' she said.

Naomi clapped her hands in delight.

'I wouldn't mind a warm bath, either,' said Victoria Stitch. 'With bubbles?' she added hopefully.

'Of course!' said Naomi. 'You'd fit right into a teacup, I would think!'

She got one out of the kitchen cupboard, moving it round slowly in her hands as though she was thinking of something.

'You know what,' she said. 'I've got a doll's house in my bedroom, from when I was little. There's loads

27

of furniture in it! Even a proper little bed. You could stay in that! Mum will never find you there, either. You'd be perfectly safe! Come upstairs! Let's go and find it!'

She beckoned excitedly to Victoria Stitch, who stood up and smoothed down her dress. Jumping onto her bloom, she followed Naomi up a staircase that creaked as Naomi walked on it.

'This is my bedroom,' said Naomi, opening a door into a brightly coloured room that led off from the hallway at the top of the stairs.

Victoria Stitch flew in, still staying close to the ceiling, and gazed around. There was a lot to take in. Pictures from fashion magazines had been tacked up all over the walls, and multicoloured lights had been strung across the ceiling. By the window was a desk with a funny-looking box on it, and there was a sequinned throw on top of the bed that twinkled in the glow of the lights. Next to the bed was a photo frame, with a picture of three smiling humans in it.

'Was that your dad?' asked Victoria Stitch, pointing.

'Yes,' said Naomi, picking up the frame and gazing at the picture fondly. 'He was the best dad in the world. I miss him so much! So does Mum.'

Victoria Stitch nodded, not quite sure

28

what to say. She wasn't used to having somebody open up to her like this. She wasn't used to having anybody talk to her at all! Except Celestine, of course.

'I'm sorry,' she said after an awkward silence. That was what you were supposed to say, wasn't it?

'It's OK,' said Naomi. 'It was a couple of years ago, now . . . It just still feels so strange that I'll never see him again.'

Victoria Stitch nodded again, biting back the temptation to tell Naomi that she felt the same way about Celestine. Her twin was lost to her forever. But still, she reminded herself. It wasn't quite the same. Celestine hadn't *died*.

'Anyway,' said Naomi, changing the subject, 'let's find the doll's house! I think it's at the back of my wardrobe!' She opened the door to a cavernous-looking cupboard and began to rummage, lugging out a large, wooden house that was painted a candyfloss pink. She heaved it across the floor and stood it against the wall at the end of her bed. Then she undid the catch and opened up the whole front. There was furniture inside, strewed about higgledy-piggledy.

'I don't have a miniature bath,' said Naomi. 'But we can put the teacup inside the house! I think it will look quite elegant. I'll go and fill it with water now!' she got up and left the room.

Victoria Stitch immediately swooped down towards the doll's house, landing on the top floor and opening up her cape to let Stardust out. He hovered in the air next to her pointed ear, flapping his tiny, leathery wings.

'Naomi hasn't even seen you yet!' said Victoria Stitch. 'But you know what, Stardust? I think we can trust her!'

She smiled, gleefully. Her first foray into the human world was turning out to be much more pleasing than she had expected.

CHAPTER 4

FOUR MONTHS LATER—WISKLING WOOD . . .

CELESTINE stared at Tiska, breathless with panic.

'What do you mean?' she said. 'Famous?'

'She's shown herself to a human!' said Tiska. 'And not just *one* human, lots of them! She's in the human newspapers and everything!'

'No!' whispered Celestine. 'How could she?'

'I don't know,' said Tiska. 'It's bad.'

The two of them stared at each other in the bright sunlight, and all around them, flowers shivered in the light spring breeze. Celestine reached out and gripped onto Tiska's hand.

'I'm so glad I sent you out to look for her,' she said. 'Getting those accelerated explorers' badges for you

31

and Ruby was worth every penny! Imagine if Lord Astrophel had got wind of this first!'

Tiska nodded. She was one of the only wisklings whom Celestine had confided in about Lord Astrophel and his controlling ways. Most wisklings would never have believed her. He was such an old and respected figure in the wood.

'It is possible other wiskling explorers might have already discovered the news by now, too,' said Tiska. 'Explorers usually try to stay away from areas heavily populated by humans, but who knows!'

'How did you find out?' asked Celestine.

'I came across it in a human newspaper myself,' said Tiska. 'It gave me a huge shock. I almost fell off my bloom! There was Victoria Stitch's face blown up out of all proportion, staring up at me from a stand outside a shop. It said that tomorrow she's going to be on show in a museum in London! The big city!'

'The big city?' gasped Celestine. 'She'll put herself and the whole of Wiskling Wood in danger! Humans aren't supposed to know about us!'

'I know,' said Tiska. 'And as soon as Lord Astrophel hears about it, he'll send wisklings out to capture her. You won't be able to keep her out of prison this time, Celestine.'

'It's probably what she deserves!' said Celestine, feeling hot anger flare up inside her. But it subsided as quickly as it had come. Victoria Stitch could be selfish and wicked, but she was still her sister. She couldn't bear to think of her in prison.

Celestine stood up and began to pace up and down the mossy grass, breathing deeply. She was queen. She had a responsibility to keep Wiskling Wood safe. Somehow Victoria Stitch needed to be stopped.

'Listen,' said Tiska. 'Even if Victoria Stitch has told humans exactly where Wiskling Wood is, they'll never be able to get into it. It's surrounded by magic!'

'I know,' said Celestine. 'But what if she tells

33

humans where the entrance and exit to our wood is? They could lie in wait, ready to capture any explorer wisklings who go in or out! None of us would ever be able to leave the wood again! We wouldn't be able to import any special ingredients or have the freedom to explore or . . .'

'I know,' said Tiska jumping up and putting a hand on Celestine's shoulder. 'But—'

'And even if she doesn't reveal the location of the wood,' continued Celestine, 'it still puts any wiskling explorer in the human world at risk. If humans are aware that sometimes we live or travel among them, then they'll be *looking* for us! Humans are so big they could squash us with one step! I've read about them in books. They tear down forests and build grey boxes to live in. They pump poisonous gases into the air. Drop bombs! Most of them don't care about nature or small creatures at all. They *eat* them! We can't risk being discovered by a race like that. They're too unpredictable. It's so much safer for humans to know nothing about us!'

'I know,' said Tiska, again, 'but listen. Apparently, Victoria Stitch has been calling herself a fairy, which, according to my research, is some sort of mythical being that humans already know about. I didn't see anything about wisklings in the article at all, and no mention of where we live. Victoria Stitch was interviewed saying that she was the only fairy allowed out of Fairyland because she is Queen and that any humans who go looking for Fairyland will be cursed. Apparently, she even showed them some magic she could do with her wand as "proof" that she has cursing power.'

Celestine couldn't help snorting with laughter. Typical Victoria Stitch.

'I suppose that does make things slightly better,' she said. 'But still. How *could* she?!'

Celestine sat down heavily on the mossy grass with her chin in her hands. Her mind was whirling. How could she even begin to protect her sister from the wiskling authorities *and* protect the wood from Victoria Stitch and her reckless ways?

'Tiska,' she said after a few moments. '*I* need to go to Victoria Stitch myself. Tell her to stop this business and go into hiding in the human world. She'll never be welcome back in Wiskling Wood again. She won't listen to anyone else.'

'What?' Tiska stared at Celestine in disbelief. Celestine had always made it very clear that she had no desire to ever leave Wiskling Wood. The human world was no place for a wiskling queen.

'It has to be me,' said Celestine. 'She won't listen

35

to anyone else. She might not even listen to me! But I have to try.'

'Right,' said Tiska. '*But*—'

'I have a responsibility to keep this wood safe,' continued Celestine.

'*But*,' said Tiska again. 'You're Queen of Wiskling Wood! You can't just leave it—they'll never let you through the gate. Let *me* go . . .'

'No,' said Celestine. 'It has to be me. I need to see Victoria Stitch. I *need* to!' Then she burst into tears.

'I thought I was never going to see her again,' she sobbed, suddenly realizing that her desire to go to the human world was about more than just protecting the wood; it was about family. 'I thought she was gone forever . . . I've wondered so many times what it would have been like if I'd gone to the human world with her instead of being Queen.'

'You did the right thing staying here,' said Tiska, putting her arm around Celestine. 'Wiskling Wood needs you. You wouldn't have been happy in the human world. Not really.'

'I know,' sniffed Celestine. 'I just miss her so much. It's like half of my heart is missing! I didn't realize it would be this hard living in Wiskling Wood without her. Especially with Lord Astrophel . . .'

'It has been easier, too,' Tiska reminded her. 'Living

with Victoria Stitch was never straightforward.'

'That's true,' said Celestine, wiping her eyes. 'But it was never boring, either. And she would never have let Lord Astrophel take over like he has done. I feel completely stifled sometimes! Please, Tiska, take me to the human world! I'm the only one who Victoria Stitch will listen to. It's the only way to protect Wiskling Wood and save my sister from prison.'

Tiska looked uncomfortable.

'If we're only gone for a couple of days, then I'm sure I can get away with it,' said Celestine. 'I'll be back before anyone starts seriously worrying where I am. I've already organized to stay with Twila this weekend, anyway. I was going to watch her dancing at the theatre. I'll send her a letter and tell her to be my alibi instead.'

'Even so, I don't see how you'll get out of the wood without anyone noticing,' said Tiska. 'They're very strict at the gate. You have to have an explorer's badge and be logged out . . .'

'Victoria Stitch didn't have a badge when she left the wood,' said Celestine. 'How do you think she did it? I still know that one forbidden spell she taught me from the *Book of Wiskling*. The sleeping spell!'

'Celestine!' said Tiska, shocked. 'You can't!'

'Oh, come on, Tiska. We can leave in the middle of

the night. I'm sure I can find a way to sneak past the guard.'

'Well maybe . . .' said Tiska, and Celestine could see that her eyes had started sparkling with excitement. Tiska loved adventure.

'Alright. Let's do it!'

CHAPTER 5

FOUR MONTHS EARLIER—THE HUMAN WORLD . . .

VICTORIA Stitch had been living in luxury at Naomi's cottage for three days now, and she hadn't left the house once. The weather had been too cold and windy for flying—or that's what Victoria Stitch had told the human, anyway. The truth was, she liked being indoors. The cottage was so warm and cosy and there was something about Naomi that Victoria Stitch felt strangely connected to. They had so many things in common. And it was much easier being in the human world with a human to look after you. She had a proper bed! And a fancy teacup bath. And a doll's house all of her own. She felt perfectly safe and hidden inside it when the whole front was closed.

Naomi had cleaned it up using a cup of hot water and a toothbrush and set up all the old furniture nicely for her. Victoria Stitch had watched, feeling a glow of warmth and happiness.

'Depending on how long you stay,' Naomi had said, hopefully, 'we could make this house really amazing! You can decorate it how you like.'

And Victoria Stitch had. She'd used her wand to magic things up, while Naomi watched on in fascination as streams of crystal sparks flurried around the rooms. Beautiful, twinkling chandeliers hung from the ceilings, soft velvet armchairs with fancy, twirly legs stood in the sitting room, and an array of diamond-encrusted crowns sat inside a special glass cabinet. Still, the things Victoria Stitch found she liked best were the things that Naomi had made for her by hand—a black quilt, sprinkled with silver stars for the bed, tiny matching cushions for the armchairs, and pretty satin curtains for the windows. Those things felt special. Naomi had also worked hard scraping off and lifting out the original rosebud wallpaper and dusty carpets. Now the bedroom was decorated in Gothic stripes, and there were black-and-white checked tiles in the hall. She had painted the bathroom midnight blue, studded with gem-like stars, and the teacup bath stood regally in the middle of the floor. Victoria Stitch liked her special teacup bath, and she had a fluffy towel that Naomi had cut out of a flannel.

'I don't expect this doll's house is as fancy or beautiful as your palace was in Wiskling Wood,' said Naomi.

'I love it,' said Victoria Stitch.

Days turned into weeks and weeks turned into months. Victoria Stitch stayed with Naomi, and Naomi stopped bothering to ask when Victoria Stitch might be leaving. When Naomi was at school, Victoria Stitch enjoyed being in the cottage on her own. She could do what she liked, as long as she made sure to keep hidden from Naomi's mum. She spent a lot of time in her doll's house, designing beautiful and eccentric clothes. Sometimes she slipped out through the letterbox and flew down to the beach to watch the waves and think of Celestine and wonder how her sister was getting on in Wiskling Wood, now that she was Queen. It was so strange to be cut off from her twin like this. Painful.

In the evenings and at the weekends, unless Naomi was out with friends, she and Victoria Stitch would spend most of their time together. Victoria Stitch would show Naomi her dress designs, and Naomi would get out her box of fabrics and try to sew them up for her. Naomi was getting better and better at sewing, and sometimes she would use Victoria Stitch as a model to try out her own designs.

'You're like my artist's muse!' she laughed one night, as Victoria Stitch posed in a floaty dress with big, scalloped wings at the shoulders, which glittered all over with sequins that Naomi had sewn on like mermaid scales.

'Well, I *am* a work of art,' said Victoria Stitch, fluttering her eyelashes.

Naomi smiled, sketching away happily before there was a sudden knock on her door and her mum walked in. Victoria Stitch just had time to hide behind the pencil pot.

'Ah!' said Naomi's mum, sounding pleased. 'You're doing homework!'

'Yes!' said Naomi. 'It's for my art project. I've decided to focus on fashion.'

'I see,' said her mum, sounding a little less enthusiastic. 'Well, don't forget to focus on your other lessons too. Don't you have maths and English homework to be getting on with?'

'Well, yeees,' said Naomi. 'But my art project is important, too! And I'm doing really well with it. Mr Miller said I'm getting really good at figure drawing now. Look!'

Naomi's mum came and looked over Naomi's shoulder.

'That is a rather good sketch,' she admitted. 'You always seem to draw the same character, nowadays—wearing clothes you've designed. Why's that?'

'Oh . . .' said Naomi, looking down at the sketch of Victoria Stitch with her dishevelled bun of hair studded all over with twinkling stars.

'She's just a character I made up.'

'Well, I do admit, she's lovely,' said Naomi's mum, and Victoria Stitch beamed behind the pencil pot.

'And these are rather good, too,' Naomi's

mum continued, picking up a couple of the tiny, eccentric outfits that Naomi had sewn for Victoria Stitch, including a stylish, shiny-black rain mac. 'Did Mr Miller tell you to make your designs in miniature?'

'No,' said Naomi. 'It was my idea. But I got extra marks for it. Honestly, Mum, I'm doing really well with my art. Mr Miller says it would be a shame if I didn't go to art school one day. He says I'm one of the most passionate students in the class!'

'I'm sure you are,' sighed her mum. 'Well, university is still a long way off. You might change your mind before then.'

'I won't!' said Naomi. 'I want to go to art school!'

'We've been over this so many times,' said her mum. 'I don't want you to make the same mistake as me. I went to art school and never made any money from my art . . . It's not a proper career option. Much better to keep it as a hobby.'

'But then I'd never have time to do it at all!' said Naomi. 'I never see you doing your shell pictures anymore.'

Her mum sighed again.

'It's dinner in five minutes,' she said.

Once she had left the room, Victoria Stitch came out from behind the pencil pot.

Naomi's face was despondent.

'You *must* focus on your art,' said Victoria Stitch. 'If it's what you want to do. *I* believe in you!'

She knew exactly how it felt to be forced to give up the one thing she really wanted.

Naomi smiled.

'Thanks, Victoria Stitch,' she said.

CHAPTER 6

ONE MONTH LATER—WISKLING WOOD . . .

'I'M going to tell Lord Astrophel that I'm leaving early to visit Twila,' said Celestine, as she stood up and adjusted her royal crown. 'Come on, he's probably in his office.'

Celestine and Tiska walked down through the palace gardens towards the back gate. Two palace guards were standing to attention: Art and Blue.

'Your Majesty.' They bowed as Celestine went through the gate, and then both fell into step beside her—Art on one side, Blue on the other. Celestine liked Art, sometimes they even chatted and laughed together, but she often wished she didn't always have to be escorted everywhere. They all walked the short way to a large, sycamore tree that stood behind the palace, which had a pair of imposing-looking doors set into the base of its trunk. Celestine didn't knock. She was Queen, and she was used to visiting Lord Astrophel here. Instead, she pushed the doors open and stepped inside, followed by Tiska and Art, while Blue stood guard outside. They were now in one large, circular room, which had a polished, diamond-patterned floor, and a huge, dark-wood desk sitting in the middle of it—also circular. Above the desk, hung a massive, glittering chandelier, its crystal drops carved into the shape of acorns. The wiskling behind the desk stood up as Celestine entered.

'Good morning, Your Majesty,' he said, bowing.

'Good morning, Silvan,' said Celestine. 'I'm just here to see Lord Astrophel. Is he in his office?'

'He is,' said Silvan. 'There's someone in there with him at the moment . . .'

'I'll go and wait outside the door, then,' said Celestine, before anyone could protest. She liked any opportunity to shake off the guards. She gestured for Tiska and Art to wait for her on the dark-wood chairs by the reception desk and then she hurried up the curved staircase alone. At the top of the staircase was a curved corridor that ran towards an imposing, heavy door with a gold plaque on it that

said: 'Lord Astrophel.' As Celestine approached she could hear murmurings coming from inside. Who was Lord Astrophel talking to, she wondered. Then she stopped, frozen to the spot. Two words had come floating through the doors. Two words that made the whole of her body stiffen and her antennae splutter with sparks.

'Victoria Stitch.'

Celestine crept forward, pressing her pointed ear to the door, straining to hear what was being said behind it.

'It's absolutely atrocious,' Lord Astrophel was saying. 'Showing herself to humans you say? Well! Never in my day . . .' He trailed off.

'Yes,' came another more timid voice. 'That's why I thought I had better come and tell you right away, sir. I left my explorer's mission immediately. Victoria Stitch must be stopped. She's putting us all in danger!'

'Quite right,' muttered Lord Astrophel. 'That wiskling has caused enough trouble to last three lifetimes. It's time we put an end to her nonsense, once and for all.'

Celestine held her breath. Her heart was beating so hard that she thought it might break out of her chest.

'News of this must not reach the Queen,' said Lord Astrophel. 'Celestine cannot find out that her sister has surfaced. It's better for everyone if she keeps believing that Victoria Stitch has disappeared into the abyss of the human world, never to be seen again.'

'But she will find out eventually,' said the explorer. 'Once Victoria Stitch is brought back to Wiskling Wood to be imprisoned.'

There was silence for a moment and Celestine felt a sharp sting of fury. She knew Lord Astrophel was sly and controlling—but *this?!*

'Things will become disordered again if Victoria Stitch is brought back to Wiskling Wood,' he said, carefully. 'Celestine will never allow her sister to be put back in prison. It would be much better to . . . deal with Victoria Stitch another way out in the human world. Without Celestine knowing anything about it. Happy Queen, happy wood.'

Celestine almost gasped out loud, and angry tears sprung to her eyes. She had a mind to push the door open and march into the room, but fear of what Lord Astrophel might do stopped her. She didn't trust him one bit.

'I need two trustworthy explorers,' continued Lord Astrophel. 'To go out into the human world and deal with Victoria Stitch. You, Salix, are one of them.'

'Me?' said Salix, and Celestine could hear the fear in his voice.

'I'm afraid you have no choice,' said Lord Astrophel.
'You already know about Victoria Stitch, and we
need to keep the number of wisklings who know
what is happening as few as possible. I am going to
surreptitiously close the gates to the human world, to
stop any more explorers going out for the time being.
And any more that come in after today will be made
to swear an oath of secrecy if they've discovered what
Victoria Stitch is up to. We don't want the news of this
getting out to the Queen or to the rest of Wiskling
Wood. It would only worry everyone. Victoria Stitch
has already caused enough damage.'

'I understand,' said Salix.

Lord Astrophel sighed.

'I'm old,' he said at last. 'I won't be around for much
longer. My aim has always been to keep Wiskling
Wood a safe and harmonious place. My greatest wish
is that it continues to be so after I am gone. The . . .
annihilation of Victoria Stitch is the only way. Don't
look so shocked, Salix!'

'I'm sorry,' stuttered Salix. 'I just . . .'

'You will be rewarded greatly for your service,' said
Lord Astrophel. 'But if I find you going against my
orders, then . . . well . . . You may find yourself facing
harsh punishment. *Life* imprisonment. I'm too old to
tiptoe around anymore. This is my last chance to rid

wisklings of Victoria Stitch. I'm not risking any half measures.'

'OK,' said Salix, in a quiet voice.

'I know of another wiskling who will help you,' added Lord Astrophel. 'Kasper. He's worked for me before. He'll be perfect for the job. He's quite . . . ruthless. I'll arrange a meeting with the two of you this afternoon and we can discuss . . . details. There are things we need to put in place. There might be . . . *spells* we could use to help us. You'll both be ready to leave first thing tomorrow morning. You say Victoria Stitch is to be on show in a human museum?'

'Yes,' said Salix.

'Find the museum,' said Lord Astrophel. 'Watch her. Follow her. But stay hidden. And as soon as you are alone with Victoria Stitch, *kill* her.'

Celestine didn't hang around to listen to any more. She turned on her heel and ran back round the corridor, tripping down the stairs to the foyer. Tiska looked up, surprised.

'That was quick,' she said.

Celestine took a deep breath, trying to hold everything together. Art mustn't be alerted to the fact that anything was wrong.

'Yes,' she said brightly. 'I realized that what I needed to tell Lord Astrophel doesn't actually matter.'

Tiska frowned, confused.

'So, let's go back to the palace,' said Celestine. 'Now.'

She hopped impatiently from foot to foot as Tiska and Art got up and made their way out of the state tree and towards the back gate of the palace gardens.

'Just so you know, Art,' said Celestine as they walked. 'I'm going to visit Twila this weekend. Ash from the front door is going to accompany me.'

'Sure,' said Art, as he opened the back gate for Celestine, letting her and Tiska inside before he resumed his station there. Celestine flashed him a quick smile and then ran off up the path, into the flowers.

'What's happened?' asked Tiska, once they were out of earshot.

'We have to leave, right now!' said Celestine. 'Lord Astrophel is closing the gate to the human world! And he knows about Victoria Stitch already! He's planning to send out two explorers to . . .' The word choked up in her throat. ' . . . kill her at the museum. They're not leaving until tomorrow morning, though. We have time to get to Victoria Stitch first and warn her!'

'What?!' said Tiska disbelievingly.

'I know!' said Celestine. 'I can hardly believe it myself. It's worse than I ever could have imagined!

But I think he's at his wits end with Victoria Stitch.' She grabbed Tiska's hand and pulled her back towards the palace and in through the front doors, where she flashed a smile at another of the guards, Ash.

'Just letting you know that I'm going to visit Twila this weekend,' she said. 'Art is going to accompany me.'

Ash bowed respectfully, nonplussed, and Celestine shot past him, dragging Tiska behind her.

'It will be a while before anyone figures out I'm not at Twila's.'

'That's all very well,' said Tiska. 'But how are you going to actually get out of the palace right *now* without one of the guards seeing you leave on your own? It's broad daylight! I'm not sure about this, Celestine. It's risky! Maybe you should just stay here and . . . expose Lord Astrophel! Tell everyone in Wiskling Wood what he's been up to! He won't be able to hurt Victoria Stitch if he's in prison.'

Celestine whirled round in shock.

'Expose him!' she gasped. 'I can't expose *Lord Astrophel!* Who's going to believe me? He's so old and respected. And Victoria Stitch is . . . not popular. Wisklings won't like that she's showing herself to humans. Besides, I don't trust Lord Astrophel. He was talking about using *spells!* If I tried to expose him, he'd find a way to wriggle out of it, I *know* he would. No, we have to find a way to sneak out to the human world. We have to get to Victoria Stitch before Astrophel's wisklings do.'

CHAPTER 7

VICTORIA Stitch paraded up and down the top of Naomi's desk, with swathes of black, glittery netting flowing out behind her. As usual, she and Naomi were designing clothes together. Regal ones. Fit for a wiskling queen. It was just a shame, thought Victoria Stitch privately, that no one else was going to see her in them. It had been three months since anyone but Naomi had laid eyes on her. Victoria Stitch was beginning to feel a tiny bit . . . restless.

'I've got to make a full-sized outfit for once,' Naomi announced, as she snipped away at the tulle fabric. 'We're doing a recycled-fashion show at school!'

'A recycled-fashion show?' said Victoria Stitch, wonderingly.

'Yes,' said Naomi. 'We all have to make a costume out of rubbish, basically. And then there's going to be a fashion show, where we all wear our costumes and walk down the catwalk! I need to think of what to make mine from. Nicola's making hers from crisp packets and Sophie said she's going to use sweet wrappers!'

'Oh!' said Victoria Stitch, and was surprised at the sting of jealousy she felt. *She* would like to walk down a catwalk with everyone looking at *her*. It had been a long time since she had felt the fizz of power from showing off.

'Yes,' continued Naomi, 'Sophie and Nicola both said . . .' She started to tell Victoria Stitch all about a conversation she had had with her friends at school, but Victoria zoned out, thinking about the fashion show. She could never go to something like that, of course. But she wished that she could! Something was beginning to stir inside her, an old spark that had mostly been dormant up until now. It had been very healing being so reverently cared for by Naomi over the last few months, after everything that had happened in Wiskling Wood. She'd had no idea humans could be so kind! But she was starting to feel a little restless now . . .

'Naomi,' she said, interrupting.

'Yes?'

'Can we go on holiday? I want to see more of the human world.'

'Oh, I'd have to ask Mum . . .' said Naomi, looking doubtful. 'I don't think we can afford a holiday.'

Victoria Stitch sighed. She found it frustrating that Naomi would never let her help with money. She had used the forbidden duplicate spell in Wiskling Wood all the time! But, she reminded herself, she *had* helped Naomi in other ways. She had encouraged her with her art to the point where her teacher Mr Miller had told her mum at parents' evening that it would be a *crime* for Naomi not to go to art school. Naomi's mum had nodded with pursed lips, but she had started doing a little bit of art again herself, creating a few shell pictures when she had a bit of spare time. She looked less tired and drawn because of it. The atmosphere in the house was altogether happier than it had been when Victoria Stitch had first arrived.

'I'll ask Mum about a holiday,' said Naomi. 'But I don't think she'll agree to it. She was talking about selling up again yesterday. I don't want to move! Dad chose this house!'

'She's always threatening to move, isn't she?' said

Victoria Stitch.

'I know,' said Naomi, 'but I saw her looking at an estate agent's brochure this morning.'

'I won't let her sell the house!' said Victoria Stitch passionately. She had grown to love the cottage. It was just as much her home as Naomi's now.

Naomi laughed.

'I don't know how you'll stop her!' she said.

Victoria Stitch didn't reply. Her mind was whirring. She carried on marching up and down the length of Naomi's desk, Stardust fluttering next to her pointed ear, enjoying the way the glittering fabric swished out behind her. She walked over to a pot and peered over the edge of it, picking out a few crystals and starry sequins. The sequins were as big as her hand! She peered

into one of them, gazing at her reflection. Large eyes outlined in smoky black stared back at her, the lids glittering with silver dust. It really was a shame there was no one else to admire her.

'What do you think would *really* happen,' she asked, suddenly, 'if the news got out that you had a wiskling, a *fairy*, living with you?'

'You said wisklings aren't supposed to be spotted by humans!' said Naomi.

'We're not,' said Victoria Stitch, dropping the star sequin back in the pot.

Naomi frowned.

'Then, why are you asking that?'

'I'm just interested, that's all,' said Victoria Stitch. 'I want to know, *hypothetically*, what you think would happen. Do you think I'd be captured and put in a cage?'

'Oh, no!' said Naomi, shocked. 'That wouldn't be allowed nowadays. It would be big news! I mean, people would be astonished! You'd probably be famous!'

'Famous?' said Victoria Stitch. She rolled the word around on her tongue. It tasted exciting.

'Yes,' said Naomi. 'But you wouldn't want that!'

'Why not?' asked Victoria Stitch. '*Hypothetically?*'

'Well, because . . . because . . . you said that it would

60

be a bad thing if humans were aware that wisklings existed.'

'Yes,' said Victoria Stitch. 'That is true. It is against the law in Wiskling Wood to show yourself to a human. But lately, I've been thinking that humans aren't as big and bad as wisklings have been led to believe!'

'Well, *most* of them aren't,' said Naomi, quickly. 'There are still bad ones about, of course! Where is this going, Victoria Stitch? I love having you as my secret!'

'I love it, too,' said Victoria Stitch. 'But think of the money we could earn! You would be able to keep this house. And I would tell humans I was a fairy. No one would ever have to know about wisklings!'

But, even as she said it, Victoria Stitch knew it was a bad idea. If she was famous then she would be breaking wiskling law. Lord Astrophel would probably like nothing more than putting her back in prison.

BUT, what if she had the humans on her side? What if there were more like Naomi out there? Kind, attentive humans who would protect her.

As she thought about it she felt a tiny explosion of fearlessness and power burst inside her chest. She missed feeling like that!

'We'd be rich!' she said. 'You and your mum would have no money problems at all! You could be my manager!'

'I don't think I'm old enough,' said Naomi. 'I'd have to tell her all about you! I don't know about this, Victoria Stitch . . . It would be a big, scary thing to do!'

'Big and *exciting!*' said Victoria Stitch, suddenly completely taken in by her idea. 'I want to do it! Oh, please, Naomi. Let's go and tell your mum about me now!'

'Now?' said Naomi, shocked.

'Yes!' said Victoria Stitch, hopping up and down gleefully.

Naomi frowned.

'You know this will be the end of our special secret,' she said.

'I know,' said Victoria Stitch. 'But it won't be the end of our friendship! That will never end. Will it?'

'Of course not!' said Naomi. 'You're my very best friend!'

Victoria Stitch glowed inside, from her sparkling antennae all the way down to her toes.

'Let's go and do it now!' she said. 'Your Mum's in! She's watching TV downstairs!' she leapt onto her bloom and whizzed towards Naomi's bedroom door.

'Come on!' she said.

Naomi stood up, reluctantly.

'Really?' she said. 'Now?!'

'Yes!' said Victoria Stitch insistently and the tips of her antennae exploded, like two sparkling fireworks.

———

Naomi pushed open the door to the cottage's cosy sitting room, leaving Victoria Stitch hovering in the hallway on her bloom.

'Mum,' she said. 'Can I talk to you about something?'

'Of course, my love!' said her mum. 'Come and sit down. I've actually got something to talk to you about, too. I want to discuss this house . . .'

'What?!' Naomi, stared at her mum in horror. 'You're not *actually* going to sell it, are you?'

'I don't want to,' said her mum. 'But we need to have a real think about it. It's just been so hard financially since Dad died and this is a big family home with a sea view. It costs a lot of money every month. I just can't keep working two jobs like I am at the moment. I'm never around for you! You spend so much time on your own. It's not right. I need to be here for you more.'

'But we can't leave this house!' said Naomi, her eyes welling up with tears. 'Dad chose this house! It was his dream for us to all live by the sea!'

'I know,' said Naomi's mum, taking her hand. 'But Dad's not here now and . . .'

'Don't sell it!' said Naomi. 'Please! Listen, Mum,

I've got something to tell you that might change your mind.'

'Really?' said her mum, disbelievingly.

'Yes!' said Naomi. 'I've been keeping a secret from you. Because I had to. This is going to sound crazy but . . . there's a fairy queen living in our house.'

'Oh, darling!' said her mum in a voice that didn't sound like she believed Naomi at all. 'I think things have really been getting on top of you lately, haven't they?'

'What?' said Naomi. 'No! It's true! I swear! Victoria Stitch, Victoria Stitch, where are you?'

Victoria Stitch came out from behind the door and whizzed into the room in a flurry of sparks.

'Look!' said Naomi, and Naomi's mum looked. Her face went white and her eyes went very, very round.

'Hello, Elizabeth!' said Victoria Stitch, hovering up near the ceiling and staring down at Naomi's mum. 'It's nice to meet you at last.'

Naomi's mum opened her mouth and then closed it again.

'This is Victoria Stitch,' said Naomi. 'She's a fairy! She's been living in my doll's house for ages!'

Naomi's mum blinked, a stunned expression on her face.

'Am I dreaming?' she asked.

CHAPTER 8

THREE WEEKS LATER—WISKLING WOOD . . .

CELESTINE pushed open the door to her bedroom, with Tiska hurrying along behind her. She wrenched open her wardrobe door and started to pull out clothes, rummaging right to the back where she knew there was a backpack stashed away. She hadn't used a backpack for years, but she and Victoria Stitch had both had one when they were younger—Victoria Stitch's had been black velvet and hers was a bright, berry red.

'There!' she said, pulling it out triumphantly and starting to throw things into it. She unpinned her crown from her head and tossed it onto the bed, then peeled off the jewelled dress she was wearing. It would not be practical for bloom flying As she did so, the door opened, and Minoux walked in with a pile of crisp, clean washing.

'Oh!' she said. 'I'm sorry, Your Majesty. I didn't know you were—'

'It's alright, Minoux,' said Celestine. 'Just put that down there.' She gestured to the bed, waving manically. Minoux glanced at Tiska, confused, and Tiska shrugged. Minoux put the washing down and peered at Celestine.

'Are you alright?' she asked.

Celestine stared at Minoux, and suddenly an idea so bold and daring fell into her head that she almost gasped. Could she trust Minoux to keep a secret? They were friends, weren't they?

'Minoux!' she said breathlessly. 'I need your help.'

'Of course, Your Majesty,' said Minoux. 'Anything!'

'I need your uniform,' said Celestine. 'Your maid's uniform. Now!'

'What?' Minoux stared at Celestine.

'There's no time to explain,' said Celestine. 'But please, please trust me. Let me wear your maid's uniform. I'll be forever in your debt!'

'But I . . .' stuttered Minoux starting to look a little afraid.

'You can just go and put on another one, can't you?' said Celestine. 'You must have spares in your wardrobe?'

'Well, yes,' said Minoux, 'but . . .'

'Please?' begged Celestine. 'I have to get out of this palace as soon as possible without the guards seeing me. If I'm dressed as a maid, no one's going to look twice! I can't tell you any of my plans, I'm sorry. You just need to trust me!'

Minoux looked wildly from Celestine to Tiska, who shrugged again.

'Queen's orders,' Tiska said.

Minoux's face had gone completely white, but she started to take off her apron.

'It's not like that, Minoux,' said Celestine, feeling guilty that she was putting Minoux in such a risky position. 'I'm asking you to help me as a friend. Not as an order.' She shot a reproachful look at Tiska.

'It's fine,' said Minoux, slipping out of her dress and apron and handing it to Celestine. 'But I'm just going to pretend I don't know anything about what's going on. Which I actually don't.'

'That would be best,' nodded Celestine, pulling on the dress and tying the frilly apron around her waist. 'All you know is that I've told you I'm going to visit my friend Twila for a few days. Just don't alert anyone to the fact that anything's amiss. In fact, I'm going to give you leave to go and visit your sister this weekend! That way you can't be incriminated. You weren't here!'

Minoux nodded, relieved, and Celestine handed her one of her long golden, royal capes, embroidered all over with silver stars.

'You can wear this to go back to your room,' she said. 'If anyone asks you why you're wearing it you can say it's a present from the Queen. It IS a present. I'd like you to have it for being such a good and loyal friend.'

'Really?' Minoux's face lit up.

'Yes,' smiled Celestine. 'Take it! I'd like you to have it! And please, please could you do me one more favour? Can you bring me your outdoor cloak? Your regulation maid's one with the royal crest on it? And the key for the maids' exit?'

Minoux nodded, wrapped her new gold-starry cape around herself, and scurried out of the door. Celestine went over to the dressing table, took off all her jewellery, and began to pin her hair into a bun.

'How do I look?' she asked Tiska.

'Not like Queen Celestine!' said Tiska. 'But you're going to have to keep your head down or wisklings will recognize your face.' She picked up Celestine's red backpack. 'I'll take this. It will look suspicious if you're carrying it. Now, where's your bloom?'

'Here,' said Celestine, opening a cupboard in her bedroom. Inside was a beautiful white rose bloom. She'd had to get a new one after Victoria Stitch had left for the human world with her old buttercup. She had thought a white rose would be ostentatious at first, but Lord Astrophel had persuaded her that it was the right sort of bloom for a queen. Celestine closed her hand around the stalk and lifted it out of the cupboard.

'Wisklings will recognize my bloom,' she said. 'Everyone knows I have a white rose. I don't think I can go through the palace gates with this.'

'That's true,' said Tiska. 'Maybe you could hide it somehow? How about in one of those big bag thingies?' She pointed towards Celestine's open wardrobe, where a few long bags hung containing her most special dresses.

'Yes!' said Celestine. 'That's perfect. If I leave the palace in a maid's outfit carrying a dress bag, I'll look just like I'm taking the Queen's dress to the tailors for repairs!'

Hastily, she heaved one of the bags out from the wardrobe and dragged it over to the bed. Tiska hurried over and together they unbuttoned it, pulling out Celestine's magnificent, heavy coronation dress and replacing it with the bloom. As they did so, Minoux came back into the room. She had changed into a new maid's outfit, and in her hands she held a dusky-pink hooded cloak with a gold crest embroidered on the back of it and a small golden key.

'No one saw me,' she whispered.

'Thank you, Minoux!' said Celestine. She took the key and put the cape on, pulling the hood up. Then she picked up the big dress bag and turned towards the door.

'I'm ready,' she said. 'Tiska, I'll meet you on the parade round the front of the palace. Minoux, please will you see her out?'

'Of course, Your Majesty,' said Minoux. She sounded bewildered, but she didn't ask any more questions. She gestured to Tiska and the two of them disappeared out of the door. Celestine waited a few moments. Then she took a deep breath and followed.

It felt strange walking through the palace dressed as a maid, and Celestine kept her head down as she hurried along the glittering corridors towards the servants' staircase, nodding briefly at any passers-by. She was relieved to find that no one paid her much attention. She went quickly down the staircase and reached the outside door that came out at the back of the palace, twisting the key in the lock to open it. There was no one in the gardens. It was a clear run to the back gate, where Art and Blue were stationed. Celestine clutched the dress bag to her chest and kept her face down as she approached, feeling her heart beginning to pound. She was glad she was wearing her hood up because her antennae were fizzing like two golden sparklers.

Surely they must sense that something wasn't quite right? But, she reminded herself as the guards opened the gates, why would they?

She looked just like a maid on her daily duties, carrying a dress to the tailors. And there was no reason for them to suspect that the Queen was trying to escape without palace protection.

'Thank you!' she squeaked as she whisked past.

Celestine scurried round the golden fence towards the front of the palace and the parade. The parade was the most prestigious street in Wiskling Wood, flanked by big oaks and beeches, with smaller turreted buildings built up between the trunks. The trees and buildings housed some of the most expensive shops in the wood, including the renowned jewellers, Goldendukes, where Celestine used to be an apprentice. She felt a sharp pang as she saw the shop. She missed having the time to work on necklaces and crowns and tiaras.

It felt strange to be out here on the parade without wisklings flocking towards her, like they'd been doing ever since she had become Queen, and she felt strangely vulnerable standing there with no guard protection. She pulled her hood down lower as she ran over to Tiska, who was waiting near the famous Buttonsponge Bakery. Together, they made their way off the parade, heading to a mossy clearing where there were clumps of wildflowers that they could sit beneath—almost hidden.

'You should change out of the maid's outfit,' said Tiska. 'Now that you're out of the palace, it will only draw more attention.' She handed Celestine the red backpack, and Celestine slipped behind a large leaf to change, putting on a spare dress and a plain black cape with a deep hood. She stuffed the maid's outfit and the key into her backpack. She didn't want to leave any clues behind. She hoped Minoux would be able to get a new key without too much trouble.

'The quickest way to the boundary exit is by bloom,' said Tiska. 'The train will be too busy.'

'I'll just have to hope no one recognizes my bloom,' said Celestine, glancing down worriedly at the dress bag.

'We'll have to risk it,' agreed Tiska. 'But lots of wisklings have white flowers for blooms. And we'll fly as high as possible. I'm sure it will be fine. Hurriedly they both unbuttoned the dress bag, and Celestine lifted out her bloom, looking around to check that there were no other wisklings about before she got onto it.

'Go!' whispered Tiska, and the two of them took off, flying vertically upwards as fast as they could. Leaves and twiggy branches rushed by in a blur, and soon they were out in the blue sky above the wood, with a carpet of trees rolling out beneath them. There were other wisklings flying about above the trees, so they kept flying upwards as high as they could go until the wisklings below them looked like little dots. There were quite a lot of them about above the area of Spellbrooke, but as they flew south it became less busy.

Celestine gripped hard onto the stalk of her bloom, feeling a strange mixture of fear, guilt, and elation. She wasn't used to breaking the rules, but what other choice did she have? It was up to her to try and protect the wood and wisklings from humans. And to save Victoria Stitch from Lord Astrophel. How could she leave her sister, her diamond twin, to *die?*

'Look!' said Celestine, a while later. She pointed to a hazy line above the trees in the distance.

'The boundary edge!' said Tiska. 'The human world is beyond!'

Celestine stared at it as they flew closer. She had never actually seen the edge of Wiskling Wood before, and she found herself feeling simultaneously terrified and excited. There were hardly any other wisklings around in the sky now—not many lived this far south—and so Celestine and Tiska flew lower, whizzing above the tops of the trees until they came right up to the hazy edge. Beyond it, Celestine could see more trees—trees in the human world—but it was as if she was looking through blurry glass. She reached out her hand and was surprised to feel that the air felt solid there. It was a strange sensation, and it sent tingles running all the way up her arm.

'You can't get through!' said Tiska. 'This invisible magic runs round the whole of the wood, and the only place wisklings can get through is at the official exit point. 'I know exactly where it is, follow me!'

Tiska dived into the foliage of the trees and Celestine followed, dodging leaves and thin branches until they were back among the trunks of the trees and slaloming through the cool, dappled sunlight near the stream. Celestine could hear it trickling nearby.

'The stream goes right through the exit gate,' explained Tiska. 'So you can leave by boat if you like.'

Now Celestine could see the stream burbling towards the edge of the wood. Above it, going right down into the water, was a golden gate. There was another gate, which was on land, to the right of the stream, and beside that was a tree-stump office. Celestine could just see through the window, where there was a guard eating his lunch.

Tiska landed a little way up from the office, and Celestine landed, too, making sure to keep out of sight of the window and pulling her hood down low.

There weren't any wisklings around, but she still felt jumpy. She stood for a moment gazing around her, noting the famous boundary wall that ran out from either side of the golden gates. It was made of piled-up stone, covered in moss, and embedded with the leftover birth crystals of all the wisklings who had come before them. It was only about waist height, but the magic stretched upwards, much further than that, becoming an invisible, hazy dome that encompassed the whole of the wood—a powerful, magic barrier to humans.

'It's beautiful!' said Celestine in awe.

'I know,' said Tiska.

Celestine gazed at the wall, twinkling and glittering in the sunshine for a few moments, envisioning how her sister would have come this way all those months ago, before suddenly snapping out of her trance.

'We'd better hurry,' she said. There might not be much time before one of Lord Astrophel's officials comes down here to close the gate.' She glanced anxiously up into the sky, as though expecting a member of the wiskling council to appear right then and there.

'You go first,' said Celestine. 'Use your badge so that you can be officially signed out of the wood. Then, when the guard unlocks the gate to let you through, I'll sneak up behind him, enchant him with the sleeping spell, and follow you!'

'OK.' Tiska nodded.

Together they made their way towards the tree-stump office. Celestine hung back as Tiska disappeared inside. She felt nervous as she stood there waiting and couldn't stop glancing up the stream and towards the sky. To distract herself, she stood on tiptoes and peeped through the window of the tree stump, willing Tiska to be quick. She could see her standing in front of a desk, smiling and laughing with the guard and then signing her name in a large book. Finally, she showed him her emerald wand and explorer's badge. At last, the guard stood up and they both walked towards the door of the tree stump, the guard jangling a pair of large, golden keys in his hand. Celestine scooted round the edge of the office, out of sight, her heart beginning to race. Was she really about to use a forbidden spell? She had never thought growing up that she would ever have cause to know or use forbidden magic from the *Book of Wiskling,* but here she was, about to use the sleeping spell for the second time. To save Victoria Stitch, yet again.

The guard walked towards the gate, followed by Tiska. He put a golden key in the big, jewelled padlock that hung down from a golden chain.

Checking around her for the last time, Celestine crept out from behind the tree stump and hurried as fast and as silently as she could over to the gate.

'There you go,' the guard was saying, cheerfully, as he swung the gate open for Tiska. 'Happy adventuring!' He sounded so polite and kind that Celestine felt bad as she raised her wand up in the air behind him and hissed the words to the sleeping spell.

'Wiskisomniosa!'

A shower of sparks shot out from the diamond star at the top of her wand, and they fell twinkling all over the guard. Immediately, he flopped forwards, and Tiska reached out her arms to grab him, cushioning his fall. Celestine helped and together they laid him gently on the ground next to the now open gate. He hadn't even had time to turn around.

'We did it!' said Celestine, gazing through the gate and feeling her breath catch in her throat. Just a few more steps and she and Tiska would be standing in the human world. Tiska held out her hand.

'Come on,' she beckoned.

Suddenly Celestine's legs felt like jelly.

'Will it hurt?' she asked.

Tiska laughed.

'No,' she said. 'It doesn't feel like anything!'

Celestine took Tiska's hand and stared out at the

wood beyond the gate. She could see trees very much like the ones in Wiskling Wood, except there were no little windows and doors in the trunks. There were no neat, paved paths and manicured, mossy patches of grass, or streetlamps, or draglets flying about. Instead, the ground looked messy, peppered with leaves and patches of mulch that no one had cleared away. There were brambles sprouting out everywhere; plants and grasses waving wildly along the edges of the stream. And what were those silvery strands and webs covered in dewdrops that hung between some of the branches? Celestine shuddered.

'Come on!' said Tiska again, and this time she pulled Celestine right through the gate.

'Wait!' said Celestine, but it was too late. They were in the human world and Wiskling Wood had disappeared behind them.

CHAPTER 9

THREE WEEKS EARLIER—THE HUMAN WORLD . . .

IT took a few days for Naomi's mum to get her head around the idea of having a 'fairy queen' in the house, and she too had reservations about Victoria Stitch showing herself to the human world.

'Your life will never be the same again,' she said. 'Being famous won't necessarily make you happy. And there are mean people out there.'

'But think of the money!' said Victoria Stitch, quite enjoying Elizabeth's reservations. This must be what it felt like to have a mother! 'I'll share it all with you and Naomi. You can keep this house! Work less!'

'I don't know,' said Elizabeth.

'Well, I'm going to do it anyway,' said Victoria Stitch, determinedly. She couldn't back out of her idea now that she had thought of it, despite the risk to Wiskling Wood and Celestine, which she was trying not to think about. She would be careful. She was desperate to feel real excitement again, the fizz of power bubbling up inside her chest. She had stars and lightning bolts inside her. Thunder, too! She wasn't meant for this quiet life.

'If it's all going to be too much for you then you don't have to be involved,' she said. 'I can handle this on my own. I'll still give you the money you need for the house.'

'Don't be silly!' said Naomi, firmly. 'You're going to need us. 'Who else knows you as well as me? Who else can you trust? If you're going to be famous, you're going to need people who really care about you by your side.'

Victoria Stitch didn't reply because her eyes had suddenly gone all prickly. Naomi had built her up again after she had been stamped on and scorned by everyone in Wiskling Wood. She really was a true best friend.

'Well, if you're sure you want to do it . . .' said Elizabeth. 'I do have a friend who knows someone who works for the local paper. Maybe that's where we should start?'

'The *local* paper?' said Victoria Stitch. 'What about the *national* paper?'

'I think we should start small,' said Elizabeth. 'The news will spread fast enough!'

'OK,' conceded Victoria Stitch, and watched eagerly as Elizabeth typed a number into her phone and rang it while Naomi watched on anxiously.

'Hello?' she said. 'Ah, Katie, hi . . .' And then Elizabeth put her finger in her ear and disappeared out of the room. Victoria Stitch didn't follow her, but she could still hear what Elizabeth was saying. They seemed to be having a catch-up and Victoria Stitch waited, tapping her foot impatiently on the kitchen table.

'Well . . .' Elizabeth said, eventually. 'I have something I want to talk to Liam about. Are you still in touch with him? Have you got his number? Ah, thank you, Katie. Yes, we really should meet up soon. Goodbye!'

Then there was silence and Victoria Stitch knew that Elizabeth would be putting this *Liam's* number into her phone. She held her breath, waiting, waiting.

'Hello?' came Elizabeth's voice. 'Is that Liam? Oh, hi! We met a couple of years ago at Katie's party . . . Are you still working for *Coastal Life?* I might have a scoop for you . . . Yes . . . Well, this might sound a little strange but . . .'

Victoria Stitch listened. Captivated.

' . . . I promise I'm not having you on,' continued Elizabeth. 'You'll have to come round and see for yourself then . . . This morning? Sure . . .'

Victoria Stitch clasped her hands together, feeling excitement bubble up inside her, along with a small stab of guilt, which she tried to push down. Things were about to get thrilling.

'He's coming over this morning, first thing,' said Elizabeth when she got off the phone. 'I'm not sure he believes me.'

'I must put on my best dress and crown!' said Victoria Stitch, and she disappeared upstairs to her doll's house, while Naomi made them all French toast for breakfast. She had become quite adept at slicing the bread very thin and cutting it into tiny two-centimetre squares, especially for Victoria Stitch.

At ten to nine the doorbell rang.

'Are you sure you want to do this?' asked Naomi.

'I've never been surer!' said Victoria Stitch, who had ordered Naomi to bring one of the fancy, miniature chairs out from the doll's house and set it up on the kitchen table on a pile of books, like a throne. She was wearing her spikiest, sparkliest crown, and a dress with a big, puffy skirt covered in sequins and glitter that Naomi had made for her. On her feet were shiny, black lace-up boots. Stardust sat regally on her shoulder.

Elizabeth disappeared and Victoria Stitch heard her open the front door. There were pleasantries, a bit of laughing, and then Elizabeth came back into view, followed by a friendly-looking man with a pair of thick, black-framed glasses on his face. He stopped dead when he saw Victoria Stitch sitting on her throne and fluttering her long eyelashes.

'But . . .' he said.

'I didn't think you believed me,' said Elizabeth. 'I don't blame you, though!'

'Well!' said Liam. 'I . . .' He couldn't seem to get any more words out; he just crept towards the kitchen table, staring at Victoria Stitch as though he couldn't take his eyes off her.

'You're . . .' he said. 'You're . . .'

'The Fairy QUEEN,' said Victoria Stitch, getting up off her throne and skipping down the pile of staggered books as though she was walking down the stairs. 'You must bow to me!'

Liam bowed, gobsmacked. Victoria Stitch looked delighted. She stuck her leg out from the puff of

FAIRY TALES

ALICE IN WONDERLAND

black tulle and did a little twirl.

'But this is huge!' said Liam, finally dragging his eyes off Victoria Stitch to stare at Elizabeth and Naomi. 'Fairies exist!'

Liam turned back to Victoria Stitch.

'You are beautiful, Your Majesty,' he said. 'Exquisite! Sparkly! Amazing!'

Victoria Stitch beamed with pleasure.

'May I take a photo?' asked Liam. 'A video?'

'Of course!' said Victoria Stitch, and she began to parade up and down the kitchen table, posing for the camera as Liam went *snap snap snap*. Her frothy black skirts dragged out behind her, shimmering and twinkling.

'People are not going to believe this!' gushed Liam. 'It's just astounding! And it's the biggest scoop our little magazine has ever had! Thanks for thinking of me!' He sent a beaming smile at Elizabeth, who sent a shy smile back at him.

Liam pressed the record button on a camera that he was carrying and they started to do an interview. He asked question after question, occasionally stopping to exclaim, 'I just can't believe this!' Victoria Stitch answered each question as best she could, steering him away from the ones about where she came from.

'I can't tell you anything about Fairyland or other

fairies,' she said. 'If I do, you'll be cursed! I'm the only fairy allowed out into the human world, anyway, because I am the Queen. You won't find any others.' Then she waved her wand sending sparks shooting from it like little fireworks.

It was almost eleven by the time Liam left.

'With news like this, I think they'll want to publish this story as soon as possible!' he said excitedly. 'Probably by this evening. Look out for a special edition tonight. Thank you, again. And, Elizabeth, I was wondering . . . if you wanted to go for a coffee sometime?'

Elizabeth blushed and glanced at Naomi, as if for permission. Naomi just stared in shock.

'Erm . . .' said Elizabeth, eventually. 'That would be lovely. Thank you.'

Liam smiled. 'Right, then! I'll call you. Oh, and one last thing. You're going to need a PR person. I've got a friend—Lily. You can trust her. She'll look after you. I'll tell her to get in touch as soon as possible!'

'Thank you!' said Elizabeth as she waved goodbye, her cheeks still slightly more flushed than usual. She came back into the kitchen, where Victoria Stitch had got onto her bloom and was flying round and round the room, making herself dizzy.

'Well, that was exhausting,' said Elizabeth, sitting down on a chair.

'Exhausting?' cried Victoria Stitch as she swirled and whirled and looped the loop. She didn't feel exhausted at all. She felt exhilarated. Euphoric. Energized! She felt like *herself*.

That evening, as Elizabeth was spooning up spaghetti bolognaise into two human-sized bowls and one wiskling-sized one, Naomi came bursting through the front door of the cottage. She had just been to the newsagent in the village and picked up a special, evening edition copy of *Coastal Life*.

'Look!' she cried, hurrying over to the kitchen table, where Victoria Stitch was just getting herself settled at a much smaller, miniature table set up on one of the place mats. 'They've put you on the front page! And every other page too!'

Victoria Stitch gazed up at the front page of *Coastal Life* and stared and stared and stared.

'It's me!' she said, a feeling of elation beginning to bubble up inside her. She looked good! Liam had photographed her posing next to a pepper pot, for scale, and she looked regal and glamorous. Spellbinding! He had even managed to capture her crown glittering in the light.

'FAIRY QUEEN ASTONISHMENT!' screamed the headline, and on the next page was the article and interview. Naomi held it up and Victoria Stitch read it, words jumping out at her. Beautiful! Astonishing! Exquisite!

'They've mentioned that I designed the dress!' said Naomi, looking pleased.

'Have they?' said Elizabeth, coming over to look. 'Oh, they have! Well done, Naomi!' She sounded very proud and Naomi glowed with pleasure.

'I'm glad they mentioned that I am the only fairy in the human world, too,' said Victoria Stitch, as she skimmed the article. 'That should stop humans looking for any more fairies. Wisklings will be safe!' She jumped out of her tiny, fancy chair and danced across the table. This was a much nicer article than any of the ones that had ever been written about her back in Wiskling Wood. Most of *those* had been scathing. This one was wonderful!

But that night, as Victoria Stitch lay in bed inside her doll's house, she felt guilt creeping over her.

She stared at the multicoloured fairy lights that Naomi had fixed onto the wall for her. They reminded her of the stars in the sky back in Wiskling Wood. They made her think of Celestine. Would wiskling explorers see the news? Would they report back to

Wiskling Wood? What would Celestine *think*?

Humans would never be able to find Wiskling Wood, though. Victoria Stitch felt sure of it. It was hidden from them by powerful magic! But still, Victoria Stitch felt uncomfortable. Humans would be on the lookout for 'fairies' now. And then . . . then, there was Lord Astrophel. He'd be furious if he ever found out she had revealed herself to humans. Victoria Stitch shivered. Who knew what Lord Astrophel was capable of?

CHAPTER 10

THREE WEEKS LATER—THE HUMAN WORLD . . .

'IT'S gone!' cried Celestine, looking behind her.
'The gate's gone! And so has Wiskling Wood!'

'Not quite,' said Tiska. 'Look more carefully!'

Celestine squinted, and now she could just about make out a hazy patch of air, shimmering ever so slightly in the light.

'That's the way back in,' said Tiska. 'If we stepped through there from the other side, we'd find ourselves back in Wiskling Wood. But we'd come back in all the way up at the north gate. The entrance. That's how the magic works. It's like a wrinkle. A sort of pocket! A human could walk across our whole world in one step!'

92

'I guess so,' said Celestine, frowning. She had never paid that much attention to her human-world studies back in school. She had never had any interest in going to the human world until now.

'Can humans see that?' she asked.

'No,' said Tiska. 'And even if they could, they wouldn't be able to get through. Only wisklings can. The magic can detect the birth crystal in our wands and the tiny chips of it in our antennae.'

She pointed to a tree trunk nearby. A tiny star had been carved onto the trunk.

'Look for the star on the tree to the left of the stream, and you'll find the gate,' she said.

Celestine nodded, feeling overwhelmed, and then jumped into the air, squealing as she spotted something crawling along the ground near to her foot.

'What is *that?*' she asked, leaping onto her bloom and hovering above it.

'An ant!' laughed Tiska. 'You'll have to get used to bugs in the human world. There are lots of them!'

Celestine paled.

Tiska got onto her own bloom and kicked off into the air.

'We'd better get away from the gate,' she said. 'Don't forget that you can sort of see through the magic out into the human world from Wiskling Wood, even if we can't see in!'

Celestine nodded again, her heart pitter-pattering in her chest. She gripped onto the stalk of her bloom and shot up into the air, disappearing into the foliage. Tiska followed.

'Let's go back to mine and Ruby's base,' she suggested. 'It's near to here. We need to make a solid plan, look at a map, and have something to eat. Lord Astrophel's explorers aren't leaving until tomorrow morning. We have time!'

'OK.' Celestine nodded.

Soon, they were both flying high above the trees in the pink evening sky, and Celestine was marvelling at the huge, feathery shapes she could see circling above them.

'Birds!' called Tiska. 'There's lots of them out here, too!'

'And those?' asked Celestine, pointing down at the grey box-like shapes she could see, now that the trees were getting sparser.

'Houses!' said Tiska. 'Humans are too big to live in trees!'

'And that?' asked Celestine, pointing to a glittering line on the horizon, reflecting pink beneath the setting sun.

'The sea!' cried Tiska, happily.

'Oh!' said Celestine, and her breath caught in her throat. It was so big and beautiful!

The two of them flew on, following the silvery ribbon of stream, which ran out from the wood and out into open countryside. Celestine could see strange, black-and-white animals with long shadows standing about below in squares of green. She could see funny, metallic contraptions whizzing along grey, winding roads. She could see the coastline getting closer and closer, pinky golden sands glowing in the evening light. She closed her eyes, feeling the gentle spring breeze ruffle through her white-blonde hair. The further away they got from Wiskling Wood, the freer she felt. She hadn't felt like this in so long! Not since before she became queen. Defiance bubbled up inside her against Lord Astrophel as she thought about how stifled he made her feel. How dare he always try to control her! And plan to kill her sister without her knowing! Since hearing him talk about using spells through the door, she was starting to suspect there was more to his methods than just being extremely controlling. He was using forbidden magic! And that made him even more dangerous. Celestine's mind cast back to all the cups of tea he had suggested she drink whenever they had a meeting. She always felt a bit strange after the tea—more compliant and willing to agree with whatever he said. No wonder she always felt as though she couldn't stand up to him!

Celestine and Tiska flew above the stream until the sun had almost set completely, following it all the way down to one of the beaches, where it finally met the sea. Celestine stared at it in wonderment. She had no idea that the beautiful crystal-clear stream she had swam in so many times back in Wiskling Wood went all the way to the sea. And the sea! It was immense! The turquoise waves rolling and cresting into sparkling white foam.

'Is this where you live?' she shouted to Tiska, as they reached the beach. It was huge and she could see a few figures milling about on the sand in the dusky light. Humans!

'Not this beach,' said Tiska, changing course and starting to fly along the coast. 'We live on a quieter beach—away from humans!' She dived down, flying lower in the air now, keeping close to the cliff face where the sea crashed against the rocks sending up clouds of salty mist.

They passed another couple of beaches until they came to a smaller one surrounded by steep cliffs and wild grass. There was a tiny stream trickling down the middle of it that must have come from somewhere else.

'This one!' said Tiska triumphantly. 'Humans hardly ever come down here. There's no path!' She wheeled in the air, following the cliff face that stuck out right into the sea. She landed on a ledge of rock right on the head of the cliff where there was a large piece of driftwood wedged firmly into a crevice. Now they were close Celestine could see that there were windows cut into the piece of driftwood, glowing with blue and green frosted glass.

'Humans can't even get around to the front of this cliff,' said Tiska. The sea never goes out that far. There's no chance of being spotted!'

Celestine landed next to Tiska, admiring the beautiful windows and noticing now that there was also a green-painted door that had been built into the driftwood front. Tiska pushed it open and beckoned her inside.

The crevice behind the driftwood entrance was larger than Celestine had imagined it would be from the outside. The uneven, grey rock had been painted white, and there were seashell sconces round the walls holding glow crystals that Tiska and Ruby had obviously brought with them from Wiskling Wood. There was a makeshift kitchen of sorts, with a funny-looking stove made from found metal. It had a stub of human-sized candle set up beneath it. Next to the stove was a sink made from an upturned clamshell and a wooden table. Right at the back of the room, behind a tinkling, shell-string curtain, was a low-down bed, and near to that, round a rocky corner, was, she presumed, the bathroom.

'Wow!' said Celestine, impressed. Tiska and Ruby's home was very basic, but it had been decorated so beautifully with lots of sea glass and pearly shells. The furniture had all been painted green with dashes of peach and red, and in the light of the glow crystals it looked very warm and comforting.

'Tiska!' shouted Ruby as soon as they entered. 'You're back already!' She jumped on her, enveloping her in a huge hug, and then jumped on Celestine, too. Celestine found herself hugging Ruby back hard. She had missed these two and their wild ways so much over the last few months.

'Wait one minute!' said Ruby. 'I'm going to get some water from the stream!' She grabbed her leaf and a shiny, red kettle from the hob and disappeared out of the door.

Celestine took off her cape and backpack and sat down on one of the chairs. Suddenly she felt exhausted. And very hungry. Tiska must have been hungry, too, because she took a jar from a shelf and opened it, offering Celestine a biscuit.

Celestine nibbled at the biscuit and looked around. There were more jars and bottles on the shelves, filled with all sorts of things: flour, sugar, and grains.

'Where do you get your food from?' she asked.

'We fish for it sometimes,' said Tiska. 'There's lots of shrimps in the rock pools. But other stuff we have to sneak from human houses and shops.' She blushed a little as she said this.

'We only take a tiny amount, of course,' she said. 'They'll never notice. It's only the same as what the explorers do when they come out to get supplies that can't be found in Wiskling Wood. You know, imported ingredients like cinnamon and cocoa and stuff.'

Celestine nodded, taking another biscuit. It tasted both salty and sweet at the same time and had flecks of something green in it.

'Seaweed!' explained Tiska. 'Ruby and I eat a lot of seaweed!'

Just then Ruby came back with the kettle, her already unkempt, dark hair looking even more windswept. She put the kettle on the stove and then lit the stub of candle with her wand. The room began to warm up and the water bubbled in the kettle. Ruby poured them all a cup of tea and then began pulling more things from a cupboard and put a big pan on

the stove to start making them dinner. The smell of soup, shrimps, fresh bread, and salted seaweed wafted through the room while the sea roared and rushed outside in the fading light.

Tiska got out a large map of the human world and put it on the table.

'This is where we are,' she said, pointing to the coast. 'And that's London, up there. That's where Victoria Stitch is going to be on show at the museum tomorrow.'

'Is it far?' asked Celestine. It was hard to tell from the scale of the map.

'It's about two-hundred and fifty human miles away,' said Tiska.

'What!?' gasped Celestine.

'Yes,' said Tiska.

Celestine stared at Tiska.

'How are we going to fly all that way?' she asked.

'We're not,' said Tiska. 'We can't. A wiskling on a bloom goes about as fast as a human on a bicycle. It would take us days. We're going to take the train. Tonight.'

'Tonight?'

'Yes,' said Tiska. 'If we leave tonight then we should get to the museum before Kasper and Salix. They're not even leaving Wiskling Wood until tomorrow morning. We'll watch for an opportunity to get Victoria Stitch alone, and we'll tell her to go straight into hiding! Or better, we'll get her to come with us! Kasper and Salix will have to go back to Lord Astrophel empty-handed! And Victoria Stitch and Wiskling Wood will be safe!'

'You make it sound easy,' said Celestine.

'Hopefully, it will be,' said Tiska.

Just then Ruby came over and placed three steaming bowls of soup and a basket of bread on the table, along with a half clamshell full of toasted shrimps, which Celestine stared at in horror.

'I can't eat those!' she said. 'They're animals!'

Tiska blushed.

'I know,' she said. 'But sometimes Ruby and I don't have that much choice over what we eat if we can't get supplies. Things are different out here in the human world.'

They all began to eat but Celestine refused to touch the shrimps. When they had finished, Tiska stood up and put on a dark green cape.

'There's a train leaving for London in half an hour,' she said. 'I looked at the timetable. We need to go.'

Celestine stood up, too, putting her cape back on and pulling the hood up. Ruby glanced at them both, biting her nails and looking worried.

'I think I should come,' she said.

'No,' said Tiska. 'I don't want you to. Stay here. Stay safe. I'll be back, I promise!' She gave Ruby a long, tight hug and Celestine turned away. She felt guilty for putting Tiska in danger like this. But Tiska was right. It would only complicate things to have the three of them navigating their way to London. There was more chance of being spotted. They made their way out onto the cliff ledge and Celestine stared out into the early evening sky as the sea crashed down below. Her insides fluttered with apprehension.

'Are you sure you know what you're doing, Tiska?' she asked. 'Will we really be safe taking the train to London?'

'Trust me,' said Tiska. 'I'm a trained explorer, remember!'

'OK,' said Celestine, taking a deep breath, trying to find the piece of Stitch that she knew was inside her. This was going to be scarier than almost anything she had ever done in her life.

'Let's go.'

CHAPTER II

THREE WEEKS EARLIER—THE HUMAN WORLD . . .

'VICTORIA Stitch!' came Naomi's voice, the morning after her photoshoot with Liam from *Coastal Life*. Suddenly the whole front of the doll's house opened and Naomi peered in. Victoria Stitch sat up in bed, her hair dishevelled, Stardust clutched to her chest.

'What?' she asked.

'You have to see what's outside the house!' said Naomi, her eyes wide and frightened. 'There are people, so many people! They've got cameras and they keep knocking on the door!'

'Cameras?' said Victoria Stitch, and she jumped out of bed, hurrying to the wardrobe to find her best dress. Fifteen minutes later, she arrived downstairs in the kitchen, where Elizabeth and Naomi were trying to have breakfast through the noise of shouting from outside. All the curtains were closed.

'Don't open them!' hissed Naomi as Victoria Stitch flew over to the window.

'I'll be careful!' replied Victoria Stitch, twitching the curtain back just a little. What she saw made the breath catch in her throat. Hordes and hordes of humans were outside. More humans than she had ever seen in one place before. They were trailing all the way up from the windows to the road outside the front gate.

'Oh!' she said and clutched onto her bloom tightly to stop herself from falling off. Suddenly she felt a bit dizzy. She flew right back over to Naomi and landed on her shoulder for comfort, just as Elizabeth's phone began to ring.

'Hello?' said Elizabeth. 'Oh, hi, Lily. Yes, Liam did say you would call.'

'It's the PR lady,' Elizabeth mouthed to Victoria Stitch, looking relieved. She put the phone on loudspeaker.

'I just can't wait to meet you, Victoria Stitch!' came a shrill, excited voice. 'I'm outside, right now! I've got a bodyguard with me, too. Can you let us in?'

'A bodyguard!' said Victoria Stitch, feeling suddenly a lot better.

Elizabeth hurried to the front door and a few minutes later there came the click of the door and the sound of voices in the hallway. A lady with sleek hair and a very bright, red-lipsticked mouth came bustling into the kitchen, followed by a large square-looking man in a black suit and sunglasses who, to his credit, didn't react at all when he saw Victoria Stitch.

'Oh!!' cried Lily, when she spotted Victoria Stitch on Naomi's shoulder. 'Aren't you just . . .' She trailed off, her red-lipsticked mouth hanging open in shock. Victoria Stitch smiled, pranced, twirled.

'I thought I was prepared,' said Lily, faintly, sitting down on one of the kitchen chairs. But, oh, my . . . How incredible!'

Her phone started to ring then and she snapped back to attention.

'I'll deal with all this,' she said to Victoria Stitch, Naomi, and Elizabeth. 'Don't you worry about a thing!'

Lily was as good as her word. She rang the police to get rid of all the people outside the house and then took phone call after phone call, chattering away in a business-like manner and writing things down in a diary. Naomi made cups of tea and arranged plates of biscuits, and Victoria Stitch pranced about gleefully, watching Lily's diary fill up with events and interviews, with Victoria Stitch as the star of the show.

'They want you on TV!' said Lily, at the end of one particularly exciting phone call. 'Breakfast TV! Tomorrow morning. Do you want to do it?'

'Yes!' shouted Victoria Stitch, without hesitation.

'Great!' said Lily, penciling it in. 'They're sending a car to pick us all up this afternoon. We'll have to stay in a hotel in London tonight. The TV company will pay.'

'Tonight?' said Elizabeth, looking worried. 'I can't come. I've got work tomorrow! And Naomi's got school!'

'But you're my manager now,' said Victoria Stitch. 'You have to come! And Naomi can take a few days off, can't she? I'm not doing any of this without Naomi!'

'I want to go!' said Naomi. 'Come on, Mum! This is a once-in-a-lifetime opportunity!'

'Elizabeth,' said Lily firmly. 'If you're Victoria Stitch's manager, then you'll be taking a cut of the fee. I wouldn't worry about missing work. In fact, you may as well give up your job altogether!'

'Really?' Elizabeth sat down on a kitchen chair, looking dazed, and Victoria Stitch glowed inside. It felt really good to finally be able to help Elizabeth and Naomi with money.

———————

A few hours later, Victoria Stitch found herself sitting in a shiny, black car accompanied by Naomi, Elizabeth, Lily, and the bodyguard. She had never been very far from Naomi's cottage or the beach before, and it felt fascinating to see more of the human world. She stared and stared out of the window as they whizzed along long, grey roads. Naomi shivered with excitement, too. She had never been to London before and had dressed in one of her self-designed outfits for the occasion—a tartan shawl that she had found in a charity shop. She had upcycled it by sewing sparkly, black pom-poms all around the edges—and with a pair of black tights, ankle boots, and large, dark sunglasses, she did look very chic.

'Wake up!' whispered Elizabeth, when they finally arrived outside the London hotel after a five-hour drive.

Victoria Stitch yawned and stretched, while Naomi blinked blearily in the cold, night air. They were ushered into the hotel through a back door and shown immediately to the best suites. There was a room for Elizabeth, with an adjoining door leading into another room with twin beds in it for Naomi and Victoria Stitch. Arranged neatly on one of the bedside tables was a fancy miniature doll's-house bed, complete with squashy pillows and soft, snowy-white blankets. There was a chocolate the size of Victoria Stitch's head sitting on one of the pillows.

'It looks like they really want to make you feel welcome!' said Naomi. 'Wow, just look at all this luxury!' She walked over to the window with Victoria Stitch on her shoulder, and together they peered out through the glass at the twinkling London skyline.

Despite it being so late, Victoria Stitch and Naomi found it very hard to sleep. It felt so different and exciting to be in the hotel room. While Elizabeth slept in the adjoining room, they bounced on the beds, did face masks in the en-suite bathroom, had a jacuzzi bath using all the luxury bubbles, and then ordered room service.

Despite ending up going to sleep at 3.00 a.m., Victoria Stitch still woke very early the next morning, fizzing with anticipation. She jumped out of bed and spent a long time getting ready in the bathroom, choosing her most glittering and regal dress, with a tulle skirt that exploded out all around her in wiskling-ish spikes. When Naomi finally awoke, they had breakfast together by the window as the sun rose, eating flaky croissants and scrambled eggs with smoked salmon. Victoria Stitch couldn't help grinning from ear to pointed ear. Right now, life felt perfect.

At eight, Lily knocked on their door and hurried them off to the TV studios with a different bodyguard following close behind them.

'I suggest you go in Naomi's bag until we get to the studios, Victoria Stitch,' said Lily. 'We'll be going out onto the pavement. News of you is spreading round the country like wildfire! We don't want to be held up.'

'Well, alright,' said Victoria Stitch, grudgingly. She slipped into Naomi's bag—a large, patent-leather one, which Naomi had found in a charity shop and styled with pompoms to match the shawl— but poked her head over the top. The minute that they left the hotel, she could see a crowd of people waiting outside the doors. People with cameras, shouting and jostling.

'Have you got her?!' someone yelled.

'Victoria Stitch! Can we have an interview?!'

'Where's the fairy queen?!'

Victoria Stitch ducked back into the bag quickly, burying herself among the clutter. She felt a sharp swing as someone tried to grab the bag and her heart flew to her mouth. Just as quickly she felt a firm pull, as Naomi yelled out and clutched the bag more tightly to her. Victoria Stitch gasped, bruised from being jostled so roughly, and adjusted her crown, which had fallen wonkily to the side. She could hear Elizabeth shouting at whoever it was who had tried to grab the bag, and through the slit at the top, she could see a fierce, bright-white flashing, like lightning. She liked attention, but this felt chaotic. Frightening. There was a lot of noise and shouting—and then suddenly silence, as a door slammed and they were safe inside the car. She poked her head back out of the bag.

'There's your first taste of real fame!' smiled Lily. 'You're going to have to get used to it!'

Victoria Stitch stared back at Lily, horrified. She didn't want to get used to *that*. Had she taken it too far? The humans outside the hotel weren't like Naomi, Elizabeth, or Lily, at all. They seemed so desperate to get hold of her.

Victoria Stitch was still shaking when she arrived at the TV studio.

'Hold me in your hand Naomi!' she demanded. 'Tightly!'

'I don't want to squash you!' said Naomi, curling her hand around Victoria Stitch as tightly as she dared.

They were shown into the studio, where Lily pointed to a big bubblegum-pink sofa in the middle of a bright room.

'That's where you'll have the interview,' she whispered. 'In an hour's time. With the presenters, Luke and Lolly.'

Victoria Stitch frowned.

'I want a special chair!' she said. 'The right size for me!'

'I believe they've found a miniature pink sofa for you,' said Lily. 'To match the big one. They're going to put it on a podium! It will look so charming!'

'It will!' agreed Naomi, but Victoria Stitch frowned.

'I want a silver chair, with twirly legs and a black-velvet cushion,' she demanded.

Lily flinched slightly, but she didn't miss a beat.

'Oh, of course, Your Majesty!' she said, pulling on the arm of a runner who was just going past.

'Victoria Stitch wants a different chair,' she said. 'A silver one with twirly legs and a black-velvet seat. Can you source one right away?'

'Uh . . . Of course, Your Majesty,' said the runner,

looking flustered. He disappeared off, and Victoria Stitch felt a surge of power rise within her as the studio became a hive of activity. Humans all around her were busying about, making things perfect for her first TV appearance. This was more like it. She felt as though she was in control again.

The TV interview went well. The two presenters fawned over Victoria Stitch and the camera panned in close to her.

'You're an absolute marvel!' they gushed. 'This is extraordinary! How tall are you, exactly?'

'Four and a half inches,' said Victoria Stitch. She had learned quickly that this was the sort of detail that humans loved knowing, and Naomi had measured her once with a ruler.

'So tiny!' exclaimed Lolly. 'And your dress is exquisite.'

'My friend Naomi made it,' said Victoria Stitch, proudly. 'She's a very talented fashion designer.'

'Fabulous!' said Luke. 'Are there more of you about?'

'Absolutely not!' said Victoria Stitch, firmly. 'I am the only fairy allowed in the human world because I am the Queen. You won't find any more of us about. And if you go looking for Fairyland you'll be cursed!'

'Oh, gosh!' tittered Lolly.

Victoria Stitch nodded gravely.

'I can do magic,' she said. Then she jumped up out of her tiny, silver chair and waved her wand, sending fireworks and sparks crackling out of it. Lolly jumped, looking nervous.

Victoria Stitch smiled wickedly and sat back down again, her black skirts puffing up around her.

Over the next few days, Victoria Stitch's life continued to be a whirl of excitement, glamour, and sparkle. With Naomi, she was whisked all over the city in shiny, black cars, given fairy-sized thrones to sit on, and presented with expensive gifts from miniaturists all over the world. She had interviews and television appearances, and photo shoots where tiny, beautiful clothes had been hastily sewn up in the finest satins and silks for her to model. She had been taken out to dinner in the fanciest restaurants and eaten tiny cakes and pastries, prepared for her by world-famous chefs. The human world was fascinated with her.

This was how it should have been in Wiskling Wood, thought Victoria Stitch. *I was a diamond baby!*

But they hadn't wanted her.

Oh, well.

The human world LOVED her!

Three days after Victoria Stitch had shown herself to the human world, she, Naomi, and Elizabeth were snuggled up together watching a film in their hotel room and eating gourmet takeaway pizza, when there was a knock on the door. It was Lily.

'There's been a very exciting offer come in for you, Victoria Stitch,' she said.

'Ooh!' said Victoria Stitch. 'What is it?'

'Well,' said Lily. 'It's a bit of a strange one, but I've had a VERY big offer from a rich businessman who wants to pay you to appear in an exhibit for a top London museum as soon as possible. He's suggesting that they build you a palace in one of their exhibition rooms—as big and as splendid as you like. And he's asking that you come and live in it at the weekends so that people can come and pay to see you in real life! *All* people want to do is see you in real life! You don't have to perform. Just live as you would in your normal . . . fairy palace, back in Fairyland!'

'Oh, no!' gasped Naomi. 'Strangers staring at you all day long. That would be horrible!'

'Would it?' said Victoria Stitch. Her eyes glittered at the thought of designing a whole palace exactly as she wished. Let them stare!

'Can I have a swimming pool? With mother-of-pearl tiles?'

'I don't see why not,' said Lily.

'I'd like a huge, glittering ballroom,' continued Victoria Stitch, 'with an enormous chandelier, made from real diamonds! And a twirly, silver bed with a star-patterned quilt! And a library full of books! And a studio where I can design clothes! And . . .'

'I suppose it *could* work if you only had to be on display at the weekend,' said Naomi. 'I've got to go back to school soon. We could spend the week at home and come up to London for the weekends!'

'Go back to the cottage?' asked Victoria Stitch.

'Well, of course!' laughed Naomi. 'You *are* going to come back home with me aren't you?'

Victoria Stitch hadn't thought much about the cottage since they had been in London, but now she got a surprising pang of nostalgia for the beach and her doll's house, with all its homemade things in it. A part of her missed swimming in rock pools and designing dresses with Naomi at the kitchen table. Besides, the idea of staying in London without Naomi by her side was unthinkable. Maybe living a quiet life down by the sea during the week and the high life in London at the weekends would be the perfect balance!

Two weeks later, Victoria Stitch, Naomi, and

Elizabeth went up to London to view the palace in the exhibition room of the museum. With so many humans working on it, it had been built in an astonishingly quick time.

'Wow!' gushed Naomi when they saw the palace. 'It's stunning!'

Victoria Stitch nodded, finding herself unable to reply because her eyes had gone all prickly. She and Naomi had been involved in the creation of the palace, talking to the model-makers and architects over the phone, but seeing it in person, finished, absolutely blew her mind. It was *beautiful!*

The palace was enormous for a doll's house, with at least twenty rooms inside, all enclosed behind glass. Chandeliers made of diamonds, emeralds, rubies, and sapphires twinkled from the ceilings, and the best miniaturists in the world had been commissioned to make ornate pieces of furniture. To the right side of the palace was a door that led outside, where a beautiful garden had been set up with faux grass and tiny bushes dotted all over with pretty paper roses. There was a mother-of-pearl tiled swimming pool, full of crystal-clear water for Victoria Stitch to swim in, with comfortable, black-and-white striped lounge chairs arranged around it. In the dressing room was a wardrobe bursting with clothes, many of them made by Naomi.

'I love it!' cried Victoria Stitch, eventually, clasping her hands together. 'I just *love* it!'

'We've installed a little door in the stand that you can go through to access the palace,' said one of the architects. 'Completely safe, as it's so small that no human will ever be able to follow you in! They can't be trusted to not want to touch you or steal you!'

Victoria Stitch paused for a moment. She hadn't given much thought lately to the fact that humans *could* be dangerous to wisklings. She'd been so carried away with all the glamour and glitter, she'd barely thought of Wiskling Wood at all. But now she felt a little tug of guilt.

'Do you want to explore?' asked Naomi, setting Victoria Stitch down on the floor and interrupting her thoughts.

Victoria Stitch found herself standing by the fairy-sized door, which was set onto the bottom left-hand side of the stand. Peering inside, she saw a dark, plain staircase, the sort you might find on the underside of a stage, that led up into the palace.

Her palace. Huge and sparkling and beautiful.

It was irresistible.

Suddenly, any last thoughts of Wiskling Wood vanished from Victoria Stitch's mind as she slipped through the door and began to run up the stairs.

She couldn't wait to explore before the opening the following day!

CHAPTER 12

THE EVENING BEFORE VICTORIA STITCH APPEARS IN HER PALACE . . .

TISKA and Celestine flew through the night towards the human train station, which was on the outskirts of the nearest village. They flew high in the sky, hoping that the coloured sparks coming from their blooms wouldn't be quite so noticeable from so far away.

'I don't know why wiskling magic always has to be so *sparky*!' grumbled Tiska.

The train station was deserted when they got there.

'We're in a rural village,' said Tiska, as they landed on top of the station roof, overlooking the tracks. 'It's not going to be like this in London, though.'

'I can't believe how enormous everything is!' said Celestine, gazing about her in wonderment. 'Just imagine how much food a human would have to eat!'

The two of them sat down on the roof and waited for the first train. The platform was deserted and when the train pulled up, with its windows glowing yellow in the night, it was easy to see which carriages were empty. They were able to fly right in without being seen. They settled themselves on the luggage rack, keeping a lookout for any humans who might step onto the train at subsequent stops.

'I can't believe we're really doing this!' whispered Celestine, as she hugged her knees tightly to her chest and shuddered at the sight of any human that she spotted through the train window. 'I can't bear to think of what might have happened if I hadn't sent you and Ruby out into the human world to keep an eye out for Victoria Stitch!'

'I know,' said Tiska, putting her hand on Celestine's knee. 'Though to be fair, if Lord Astrophel's plan had gone smoothly, you would never have known anything about this, anyway. You would always have just thought she had disappeared into the human world, never to be seen again.'

'That's true,' growled Celestine, a fresh burst of anger flaring up inside her at Lord Astrophel's sly and underhand ways.

The train trundled on through the night. At one point, two humans got into the carriage. Celestine felt herself tense as she watched them sit down. They got out two rectangular objects that shone with a white light.

'Don't worry,' whispered Tiska. 'They'll be absorbed in those for the rest of the journey.'

'What are they?' asked Celestine.

'Phones,' said Tiska. 'Human magic!'

It took over five hours for the train to arrive in London. Celestine could feel herself getting tired, but she didn't dare close her eyes. More humans got onto the train the closer they got to London, although the carriage still wasn't full.

Eventually, an hour before midnight, they pulled in at a huge station with a domed roof. Through the windows, Celestine could see other trains pulling in on other tracks.

They both watched as the humans in the carriage stood up, stretched, and made their way off the train.

As soon as the carriage was empty, Tiska said, 'Now! Go!' and she jumped astride her bloom and whizzed out of the door, flying vertically until she was right near the domed ceiling of the station. Celestine followed and together they peered down from their high vantage point.

'No one saw us,' said Tiska. 'Humans don't usually bother looking up.'

'Wow!' gasped Celestine, once they were through the station exit and hovering up in the cold night air above the city. Lights stretched out as far as she could see, strings and strings of them running along the edge of streets and roads, which were still busy even at this time of night. Windows glowed with yellow light from shops that were still open and from tall buildings that stretched up towards the sky. There were humans hurrying this way and that among the vehicles that crawled along the roads, their engines hissing and growling, headlights shining and horns tooting.

'Horrible isn't it!' said Tiska.

Celestine didn't reply. She was mesmerized. It was a world away from the tranquility and nature of Wiskling Wood.

'You think it's busy now,' said Tiska. 'But if this was daytime . . .' She trailed off and held on to her bloom with one hand while shaking a map of London out to look at it.

'South,' she said. 'We need to fly south to the museum! Across a big park!'

Celestine followed Tiska, still gaping at everything

she could see down below. She was surprised at how safe she felt flying above this human city. But they were so high up above it there was no chance of being spotted, and besides, from what she could see, humans all walked with their heads down, preoccupied with their phones or hurrying fast to get somewhere.

'There!' shouted Tiska once they had crossed the park and flown over a few more streets. She pointed to a very large, fancy-looking building with wide steps running up to a huge, arched entrance. It was wreathed in darkness, a silent brooding beast.

Celestine stopped in the air, her eyes wide with shock. Pasted across the whole front of the building was a huge poster with a picture of Victoria Stitch's face on it, blown up to gigantic proportions.

'Wow!' breathed Tiska, and her voice was full of dread. 'Look at that!'

Celestine shivered. It was eerie seeing Victoria Stitch like this, grinning back wickedly at her through the dark. She shouldn't be there! On display like that for all the human world to see! The gravity of what her sister had done suddenly hit Celestine, full force, and she almost let go of her bloom stalk.

'Come on,' said Tiska, after a moment. 'Let's not waste time. 'We have to find the exhibition room that Victoria Stitch's palace is in. Then we'll sit and watch

and work out a way of getting to her.'

'How will we find her room?' said Celestine. 'The museum is so big!'

'I think we should fly around the edge of the building and look through the windows,' said Tiska.

The two of them began to make their way around the building, peering in through the dimly lit windows. They could see shadowy shapes inside, statues that made them jump, and strange artefacts that looked almost sinister in the gloom. At one point, they saw a security guard with a torch, patrolling about in a long hallway. Eventually, they came to a big, arched window quite near the entrance on the first floor. Celestine felt her heart leap up to her throat as she peered inside.

'There!' she said. 'Tiska, that must be it!'

Tiska joined Celestine, and they pressed their foreheads to the glass. Inside a very large room was a huge, ornate palace, built in the style of a doll's house. It had a whole open front that humans could see into, behind glass.

'Do you think she's in there now?' asked Celestine.

'I don't think so,' said Tiska. 'In the article I read, it says that she's just going to be on show during the weekends. I don't know where she lives the rest of the time. All I know for sure is that Victoria Stitch will be in this exhibition room tomorrow!'

The two of them alighted on the flat top of a tall pillar to the left side of the arched window.

'This is the perfect place to wait,' said Tiska. 'It's high up enough that no humans will spot us from down below, and we can peer into the window to watch for Victoria Stitch! I'll get some leaves from that tree nearby to cover us, just in case Salix and Kasper arrive at the museum earlier than we think they're going to. It won't do for them to see you out in the human world, Celestine!'

Celestine shivered at the thought of Lord Astrophel finding out that she knew about his plans. If that happened, he'd want her dead too. She knew it.

'They're not planning to leave Wiskling Wood until tomorrow morning,' she reminded Tiska.

'I know,' said Tiska. 'But what if they've changed their minds and left already? We can't be too careful. We'll take turns to keep a watch of the sky while the other sleeps. We'll be sure to spot Salix and Kasper's leaf sparks in the darkness if they turn up at the museum tonight. It will give us time to hide.'

'OK,' said Celestine. 'You can sleep first if you like. I feel too jumpy! I can't stop thinking about what will happen when we finally get to speak to Victoria Stitch. I'm worried she won't listen to us!'

'Of course she will!' said Tiska. 'She has to! Unless she wants to *die*!'

Celestine felt her insides twist up at the thought.

'Mmm,' she said. She knew Victoria Stitch better than anyone. She knew there was a possibility that her sister wouldn't back down. Maybe not even for the good of Wiskling Wood. At that thought, Celestine felt a familiar spark of anger ignite within her. Sometimes Victoria Stitch could be *infuriating*.

After Tiska had collected some leaves to disguise themselves with, she laid her head down in Celestine's lap. Celestine opened up her backpack and chewed on a strip of salted seaweed, keeping her eyes wide open and trained on the moonlit sky. Three hours passed. When Celestine's eyes started to feel heavy, she shook Tiska awake and they switched over.

By the time Celestine awoke from a troubled sleep, the sun was beginning to rise in the sky and she was shocked to see a huge crowd of humans waiting outside the front entrance to the museum. There were hundreds—no, *thousands* of them!

'Oh, my goodness!' she squeaked, shuffling right to the back of the pillar, beneath the tent of leaves that Tiska had made for them.

'It's OK,' said Tiska. 'They can't see us from down there.'

'Ooh!' said Celestine, suddenly. 'Look!' she pointed through the large arched window. A movement inside the museum had caught her eye. A woman and a girl had walked into the big exhibition room. The girl was carrying a big stiff handbag which she set down on the floor.

Appearing over the top of the handbag came an ornate-looking crown, twinkling with tiny stars. Then a tiny face popped up, grinning gleefully, eyes ringed darkly in black kohl. Celestine's heart caught in her throat, and for a moment she felt dizzy with the surrealness of it all. It was Victoria Stitch!

Her sister!

Her diamond twin!

Troublemaker.

Celestine watched, transfixed, as Victoria Stitch swung her leg over the top of the handbag and slid down the shiny outside. She was wearing pointed boots with silver stars on the toes that matched the glittering, silver crown perched on top of her head. Stardust fluttered by her ear. Stardust! Celestine had missed the little draglet. Her heart tightened up with love and fear.

Victoria Stitch smiled up at the girl, and they said something to each other. Celestine couldn't believe how boldly her sister was behaving. She was talking to a human. Talking to one! Smiling! Were they friends, even? Despite herself, she felt a sting of jealousy.

Victoria Stitch looked around her, but it seemed as though she knew exactly where she was going as she headed towards the bottom left side of the platform beneath the palace and slipped through a little wiskling-sized door that Celestine hadn't noticed before.

Celestine held her breath as she watched Victoria Stitch disappear for a moment and then reappear inside the palace, behind the glass. She waved excitedly at the girl and the girl waved back. She looked happy, gleeful, and in control. Celestine recognized that look in her sister, though she hadn't seen it for a long time. It meant that Victoria Stitch felt *powerful*.

Celestine gulped.

Victoria Stitch feeling powerful was not a good sign. It paved the way for danger and recklessness.

More importantly, it meant that her sister would be unlikely to listen to anything that Celestine had to say.

Victoria Stitch began to skip through the palace at the same time as the museum entrance doors opened and the humans who were waiting outside began to surge forward.

CHAPTER 13

IT was the first weekend of appearing in her show palace, and Victoria Stitch was so excited! She ran straight into the grand dining room and sat down at the table, admiring for a moment the scaled-down images of the magazine covers she had modelled for, which were framed on the walls in twirly rococo frames. There was her favourite, the *Vogue* one of her posing, draped over a hugely expensive and glittering human-sized diamond necklace.

Victoria Stitch then turned to the feast that had been set out on the table. Flaky, miniature croissants had been displayed beautifully in a basket. There was a tiny fruit salad, pots of butter, lemon curd, and blackberry jam—and pancakes the size of human

pennies, stacked up, fat and golden. Victoria Stitch tucked in, just as the first human face peered in at her through the glass. It made her jump! She gathered herself, waving royally before continuing to eat her breakfast. It wasn't long before the entire stretch of glass along the front of the palace was taken up with human faces, staring in at her in disbelief. Victoria Stitch gulped, feeling a little more self-conscious than she had expected under the extreme scrutiny.

Suddenly, there was a blinding flash, and Victoria Stitch let out a surprised squeal. What was that?! *Oh!* One of the humans was taking photographs of her! She hadn't been expecting that. There was a clear 'No photography allowed' sign, right by the palace.

Victoria Stitch frowned and jumped up from her chair, waving her tiny fist at the human and shouting, but there was no way of the human hearing her through the soundproofed glass. Instead of looking sorry, the human laughed!

They *laughed!*

Victoria Stitch tried to ignore the unpleasant feeling that suddenly surfaced within her, taking her by surprise. She almost felt like she was back at school again, being made fun of by the other wisklings.

She glared through the glass at the human, pleased to see a security guard appear and reprimand them for taking photos.

Victoria Stitch huffed and sat back down at the table. She had a hunch that this probably wasn't the last time that a human would do something she didn't like.

———

After a large breakfast, Victoria Stitch felt a lot better. She hurried up her magnificent staircase to her dressing room, where she slipped behind a curtain and put on her black-and-white striped swimsuit. She reappeared, skipping down the staircase, preening and twirling, before making her way 'outside' to the miniature pool. It looked so inviting with its aqua-blue water, and she splashed in, swimming a few lengths in front of the humans before getting out and having a cocktail on one of the lounge seats. It didn't really seem to matter what she did. The humans were fascinated, their giant faces staring in at her through the glass in absolute wonderment, as they queued and jostled to get a look at her.

And so the day went on until it was five o'clock and the last human face had goggled in through the glass. The doors to the museum closed, and Victoria Stitch made her way wearily back down the small hidden staircase to the tiny door that led out into the great exhibition room, where Naomi was waiting for her with the handbag. She jumped gratefully in. It had been an exciting day, but being on show for eight hours had taken its toll and she felt drained. She was looking forward to spending some alone time with Naomi. A human who actually cared about her.

CHAPTER 14

'I can't believe her nerve!' said Celestine, as she watched Victoria Stitch climb onto the girl's hand. She and Tiska had watched Victoria Stitch's antics through the window all day, lying on their fronts on top of the pillar, while also keeping watch for Lord Astrophel's explorers from the safety of their leaf tent. There hadn't been a single opportunity all day to get close to Victoria Stitch, and Celestine had felt panic rising with each passing hour. The longer it took for them to get to Victoria Stitch, the more chance there was of Salix and Kasper turning up and getting to her first.

'I suppose, even if they left Wiskling Wood early this morning it could take them a good six or seven hours to get all the way to the museum,' said Tiska. 'Let's just hope they're still on their way to London.'

Now it was the end of the day, and Celestine watched her sister hop back down into the handbag. She looked exhausted, Celestine thought. Paler than usual, and drawn. Her crown was crooked on her head and she hadn't even bothered to fix it. As Victoria Stitch disappeared from view, Celestine felt her heart tighten.

'We have to follow her!' she said. 'It might be our only chance to get her alone! If we're lucky we can

whisk her away before Salix and Kasper even turn up!'

'Yes!' said Tiska. 'Let's just hope they're *not* already here, and we just haven't spotted them.'

Celestine felt a chill creep over her body as she looked around at the bright blue sky, the trees in the forecourt of the museum, and all the humans milling about beneath them. Salix and Kasper could be hiding anywhere and waiting for the perfect moment to pounce. It made Celestine shiver with fear.

'Come on Tiska, let's follow the human carrying Victoria Stitch in her bag.'

The two of them jumped onto their blooms and rose up into the sky, flying high above the museum. They watched and waited until they saw a movement down below. A back door opened and the handbag girl hurried out, getting straight into a shiny black car that was waiting for her.

'How are we going to keep up with a car?' Celestine asked in despair.

'It's the city,' said Tiska. 'There's so much traffic, the car won't be able to go that fast. We'll be able to keep up; just make sure you stay high in the sky. There are so many humans around now!'

Celestine and Tiska followed the car as it moved into a stream of traffic, inching up a street that was heaving with humans all scurrying about. Eventually, the car pulled up outside a large, fancy-looking building, where there was a big crowd of people all waiting on the pavement outside. A man in a suit got out of the car and roughly pushed through the crowd, making a path for the girl.

'This must be where she's staying,' said Tiska. 'It's a hotel! We need to peep in at the windows again. Like we did at the museum. It will be the safest way to locate Victoria Stitch's room!'

They descended, and slowly and stealthily began to fly along the outside walls of the hotel, starting with the highest windows first. They mostly just saw empty rooms with neatly made beds in them, but at last, they came to an open window on the seventh floor, from which music was blaring. Celestine had never heard music like it before. It made her toes twitch and her antennae spark. She peered into the window and gave a little gasp. There was Victoria Stitch.

'It's her!' she hissed, pulling Tiska close and jabbing her finger in the air. 'We've found her!'

The sense of elation was immense, made even sharper by the euphoric music that she could hear coming from the TV inside the room. Victoria Stitch was watching the television, jumping up and down and dancing, her hands in the air and her eyes closed, a big cherry-pink smile on her face. Her antennae were fizzing like two silver fireworks. She looked so wildly, unabashedly happy. The human girl was sitting on the bed, watching Victoria Stitch with a fond expression on her face. Eventually, the music stopped and Victoria Stitch threw herself down backwards onto the huge expanse of bed. The human laughed and Celestine felt her heart tighten. She could tell from their body language that the human and Victoria Stitch were close. They were friends. Real, proper friends.

After a while, the girl got up and stretched, disappearing into the en-suite bathroom, closing the door behind her.

Celestine stared at Tiska, and Tiska stared back with a wild look in her eyes.

'It's now or never,' she hissed. 'Let's go!'

CHAPTER 15

CELESTINE's heart felt like it was about to explode out of her chest, as she and Tiska wheeled through the open window and into the hotel room on their blooms. Victoria Stitch was still lying, splayed out on the bed, staring happily at the ceiling. Celestine and Tiska flew right over her, the green and silver sparks fizzing out from their blooms and dissipating in the air above Victoria Stitch.

Victoria Stitch stared upwards. Her eyes becoming round like saucers. She let out a small squeal as Celestine dive-bombed towards her, landing on her and enveloping her in a huge, tight hug.

'Celestine?' gasped Victoria Stitch.

'Victoria Stitch!' cried Celestine. Tears sprung to

her eyes and began to roll down her face. 'I thought I might never see you again!'

Victoria Stitch stared at Celestine in shock, her antennae crackling with the fiercest diamond sparks, interspersed with shots of hot pink and acid green. There were tears in her eyes too.

'Oh, Celestine,' she said at last. 'What are you doing here? You shouldn't be here!'

'Nor should you!' retorted Celestine, finally letting go of Victoria Stitch and stepping back. 'What are *you* doing here?'

Victoria Stitch shrugged, catching sight of Tiska now and raising her arched eyebrows. The two of them had never seen quite eye to eye.

'You're in danger, Victoria Stitch. Lord Astrophel is after you!' Celestine said, breathlessly.

'What?!' said Victoria Stitch, her heart sinking like a stone. 'But why?!'

'Why do you think?!' said Celestine. 'You're a danger to Wiskling Wood!'

'I'm not!' Victoria Stitch insisted. 'I've told everyone I'm a fairy. No one knows I'm a wiskling! Why can't Lord Astrophel just leave me alone! He's got you as Queen now. I don't understand why he always has to try and ruin my life!'

'It doesn't matter that you've told everyone you're a fairy,' said Celestine. 'Humans will now be on the lookout for tiny beings like us! You didn't really think you could get away with this did you?'

'I . . . I don't know,' mumbled Victoria Stitch, hanging her head. 'I didn't let myself think about it too much.'

Celestine shook her head in exasperation.

'Well, you have to stop,' she said. 'Go into hiding! You're putting all wisklings in danger, and Lord Astrophel wants to *kill* you!'

Victoria Stitch felt chills run all the way up her body.

'No!' she said. 'He wouldn't go that far!'

'He would,' said Celestine. 'I heard him plotting it in his office. He's sneakier than you think, Victoria Stitch. I thought I'd have the ultimate power becoming Queen, but it's not like that at all. Lord Astrophel controls *everything*.'

Victoria Stitch frowned.

'That doesn't sound right,' she said.

'It's not,' said Celestine. 'I don't know what I can do about it. But there's not time to talk about that now. Lord Astrophel's sent explorers out on a secret mission! They're going to go to the museum, watch you, and follow you. Luckily, Tiska and I got to you first!'

'His explorers will never get to me,' scoffed Victoria Stitch, even though prickles were running all the way up and down her arms. 'I'm always surrounded by humans!'

'Of course they'll be able to get to you!' said Celestine. 'Look how easy it was for me and Tiska to get to you!'

Victoria Stitch didn't say anything, but Celestine could tell she looked a bit spooked.

'That aside,' said Celestine angrily, 'you're putting the whole of Wiskling Wood in danger! You have to stop this. Come with us now and we'll find somewhere safe for you to hide. I can protect you, Victoria Stitch, but you have to come now!'

There came a flushing sound from the bathroom and Tiska grabbed onto Celestine's arm.

'We have to go!' she said.

'No!' said Victoria Stitch, gripping onto Celestine suddenly and holding her so tightly that her fingernails dug in. 'Don't go! You've only just arrived!'

'Come with us, then!' said Celestine, trying to shake herself free. 'We can't be seen by a human! Come with us! Now!'

'Naomi's safe!' said Victoria Stitch. 'She'll never tell anyone about you. Oh, please stay!'

'No!' said Celestine fiercely, finally managing to tear herself away from Victoria Stitch's grasp. 'Just because you don't mind being seen by a human doesn't mean that the rest of us don't care! Wisklings are never supposed to be seen!'

There came the sound of running water from the bathroom and Celestine jumped onto her bloom, hovering up in the air above the bed.

'Listen to me!' she hissed, desperately now. 'You're in danger. Come with me and Tiska!'

Victoria Stitch crossed her arms over her chest, defiantly.

'No!' she hissed back. 'I don't want to! And I don't want to leave Naomi either.'

'But you HAVE to!' said Tiska. 'You're putting wisklings in danger! And yourself. Lord Astrophel wants you dead!'

'I'd rather be dead, then!' said Victoria Stitch, obstinately, but there were two pink spots on her cheeks and she was blinking too fast. 'I like it here. I'm respected here! Humans love me. I feel like I belong. I'm *happy*!'

The door to the bathroom clicked and began to open. There was no time to say anything else. Celestine and Tiska shot through the air, back towards the open window, flying all the way up into the sky and landing on the roof of the hotel, out of sight.

'Just in case Victoria Stitch follows us to the window with the girl,' Tiska said breathlessly. 'We can't risk being seen!'

Celestine sunk down onto the roof tiles with her head in her hands.

'That wasn't how it was supposed to go,' she sobbed.

'I know,' said Tiska, putting her arm around Celestine.

'I've come all this way to find her . . .' said Celestine. 'After so long! And she just . . . she just . . . Oh, I should have known better! Victoria Stitch never does anything she's told. She's so selfish!'

CHAPTER 16

VICTORIA Stitch stood on the bed, staring straight out in front of her. Her face was snowy white. She almost couldn't believe what had just happened. It seemed absurd that Celestine had been here just a moment ago.

'Are you alright?' asked Naomi, coming into the room. 'You look like you've seen a ghost!'

Victoria Stitch swallowed, trying to force a smile.

'I'm fine,' she said in a bright, high-pitched voice.

'Are you sure?' Naomi frowned.

'Yes,' squeaked Victoria Stitch. 'I'm just tired.' Then she flopped back down on the bed and stared straight up at the ceiling.

So, Lord Astrophel wanted to *kill* her, did he?

Victoria Stitch felt the old, angry flames beginning to consume her. How dare he! How dare he! Didn't he realize how famous and important she was in the human world? Millions of humans knew her name. She was the fairy queen in this world. He had ruined her life in Wiskling Wood, and now he wanted to come and ruin her life here, too! Victoria Stitch growled.

But then there was Celestine . . . Her sister had risked her life coming to warn her about Lord Astrophel, and what had she done? Pushed her away. Victoria Stitch felt a sting of regret. If only Celestine had been able to stay longer, they could have talked properly.

Victoria Stitch sat up and shivered, glancing at the open window. Were Lord Astrophel's explorers out there right now? Was *Celestine* still nearby?

Victoria Stitch jumped onto her bloom, grabbed her wand, and whizzed over to the window, flying outside into the cold night air. She gazed about wildly, but Celestine was nowhere to be seen. With her heart heavy in her chest, Victoria Stitch flew back into the room and landed on Naomi's shoulder. It was too late. Celestine had obviously gone back to Wiskling Wood and left her here.

But Lord Astrophel's explorers could be anywhere.

'You had better close the window,' she said to Naomi.

CHAPTER 17

THAT night, Victoria Stitch lay in bed with her big eyes wide open, staring into the darkness. Naomi was asleep and Elizabeth had come to say goodnight long ago, poking her head round the adjoining door between their rooms. The curtain had been drawn against the closed window, but there was a tiny chink of moonlight coming through from outside. Now that it was so quiet and still, Victoria Stitch's mind turned solely to thoughts of Celestine. It had felt amazing to see her sister again for those few moments, and she regretted now the way that she had acted—so obstinately. Celestine must have risked a lot to come all the way to the human world.

Victoria Stitch wriggled out of bed and picked up

her bloom. She flew back over to the closed window, golden sparks trailing from the buttercup, which had once been Celestine's bloom. She approached the gap in the curtains, slowly, peeping gingerly just in case Lord Astrophel's assassins were waiting out there on the windowsill. There was nothing. She slipped through the gap in the curtains and landed on the inside sill, peering through the glass near the bottom. What she saw made her breath catch in her throat. Right down near the corner, was a face peering through from the other side in the darkness. A face framed by silvery-blonde hair, shining white in the moonlight. It was Celestine!

Victoria Stitch had to stop herself from gasping out loud. She put her hands up to the window, pressing them hard into the cold glass, wishing she was strong enough to open it. Celestine put her hands up too, perfectly mirroring Victoria Stitch's. Celestine opened her mouth and started to say something, but Victoria Stitch couldn't hear through the glass. She took her hands away and reached for her wand, remembering a simple spell she had learned from the *Book of Wiskling*. Muttering an incantation under her breath, she began to write in the air with her wand, leaving a silvery sparkling trail that shone in the air before dissipating.

I LOVE YOU.

I'M SORRY.

Celestine smiled.

'I love you, too,' she mouthed.

Victoria Stitch continued to write.

CAN WE TALK?

Celestine nodded her head, vigorously.

YOU CAN TRUST THE HUMAN, wrote Victoria Stitch. PLEASE LET ME GET HER TO OPEN THE WINDOW.

Celestine shook her head.

'No!' she mouthed, her eyes filling with horror.

PLEASE, wrote Victoria Stitch. I TRUST THIS HUMAN WITH MY LIFE. YOU CAN, TOO. SHE

KNOWS ABOUT YOU.

Celestine frowned, her antennae sparking with a mixture of fear and fury. She looked down towards her feet, and now Victoria Stitch could see that Tiska was there, too, just below the frame of the window, curled up asleep on the outside sill. Celestine gesticulated wildly at Tiska, shaking her head. Victoria Stitch understood what she was saying. Even if Celestine agreed to been seen by Naomi, Tiska never would. Tiska was a wild thing, a trained explorer. She had taken an explorer's oath.

Celestine gently nudged Tiska.

DON'T WAKE HER! wrote Victoria Stitch. But it was too late. Tiska was stirring, her long green, wild hair shining like waterweed in the moonlight. She opened her eyes blearily and then saw Victoria Stitch. Celestine said something and Tiska looked angry and shook her head fiercely at Celestine, pointing at her explorer's badge.

Celestine gazed back at Victoria Stitch, shaking her head.

'No,' she mouthed.

But now Victoria Stitch could hear Naomi stirring in the bed nearby. Maybe the light from her wand had disturbed her.

'Victoria Stitch?' whispered Naomi, through the

darkness. 'Why are you at the window?'

Feeling guilty for betraying her sister but not knowing what else to do, Victoria Stitch put her hand up to her mouth for a moment, shielding her lips from Celestine.

'Open the window, Naomi,' she said. 'Quickly!'

Naomi slipped out of bed and hurried towards the window. Victoria Stitch saw Celestine and Tiska gasp in horror as the human girl suddenly loomed up in front of them. Quick as a flash, Tiska jumped onto her bloom and disappeared beneath the sill, but Celestine stayed where she was, gazing back in utter terror.

'Oh my goodness, more wisklings!' said Naomi as she hurriedly heaved the stiff, sash window open. Immediately Victoria Stitch slipped out onto the sill and grabbed onto her sister's arm.

'You *did* tell humans about us!' gasped Celestine.

'Only Naomi,' said Victoria Stitch. 'And she doesn't count. I promise! Don't go, Celestine! Please!'

CHAPTER 18

CELESTINE didn't say anything further, just stood there as though stuck to the stone sill, her face a deathly white.

'Celestine!' said Naomi, her eyes dancing with enchantment. 'You're Victoria Stitch's twin! The Wiskling Queen!'

Still, Celestine said nothing. She was shaking all over with anger and fear.

'I won't hurt you, Celestine,' whispered Naomi. 'I promise!'

Celestine swallowed.

'Tiska!' she managed after a moment.

'I'm sure she'll be back in a minute,' said Victoria Stitch. 'Come inside for a bit!'

'I can't come in!' said Celestine, visibly shocked.

'Of course I can't!'

'But it might be dangerous out here,' said Victoria Stitch. 'You said yourself that Lord Astrophel's explorers are after me.'

'That is true,' said Celestine, glancing fearfully up at Naomi and then back out at the sky. She looked torn. After a moment, she very reluctantly stepped over the threshold and into the hotel room. Naomi gently closed the window behind her and stepped back so as not to frighten Celestine further.

Celestine took a deep breath and turned to Victoria Stitch, avoiding Naomi's gaze. Her antennae were now fizzing with furious, icy sparks. She clenched her hands into fists and said, 'You have to do what I say. Let Tiska and I hide you. Do you want to die?'

'No,' whispered Victoria Stitch, her shoulders slumping. 'But I don't want to have to hide, either! Why should I?'

'Because you're putting wisklings in danger!' said Celestine, exasperated. 'And yourself!'

'But I've told humans I'm a fairy!' argued Victoria Stitch. 'Except Naomi, of course. But you can trust her, I swear!'

Celestine shook her head in frustration.

'You know that saying you're a fairy makes no difference, really,' she said. 'Humans will still be on the lookout. It puts us all at risk. Especially explorers!'

Victoria Stitch had the grace to look guilty.

'Not all humans are bad,' she said, glancing up at Naomi.

'But not all humans are good, either,' said Celestine. 'It's just too risky for humans to be aware of us.'

'Does the rest of the wood know what I've done?' asked Victoria Stitch in a quiet voice.

'No,' said Celestine. 'Lord Astrophel is going to try and cover it up. He's worried the news would cause complete panic.'

'Gosh!' interjected Naomi, tentatively. She had been listening in awe. 'I didn't know you were in this much trouble, Victoria Stitch. You need to listen to your sister! You can hide at the cottage. It's not like

we need the money anymore. You've earned enough to buy a hundred cottages! Let's go back to how we were before.'

Victoria Stitch gasped, glaring up at Naomi.

'You can't side with Celestine!' she said. 'You're meant to be my friend!'

'I *am* your friend,' said Naomi. 'That's why I want you to be safe.'

'It's not about sides,' said Celestine, smiling gratefully at Naomi and relaxing in her presence a little more.

'I don't want to hide!' repeated Victoria Stitch.

Celestine's eyes shone with angry tears.

'Lord Astrophel WILL find you,' she said.

'But I don't want to live my life in hiding,' said Victoria Stitch, her eyes filling with tears too. 'I want to be me! The glorious glittering me! I can't do that if no one can see me! People like me here, Celestine! They *adore* me!'

Celestine gave a watery smile.

'But what you're doing is coming at such a great cost,' she said. 'To Wiskling Wood and to yourself.'

'Well, if they find me, they find me,' said Victoria Stitch, obstinately. 'I'd rather burn brightly and quickly, like a firework, than never burn at all!'

'Oh, Victoria Stitch!' said Celestine, as tears ran

down her face. 'How can you say that!'

Victoria Stitch shrugged, staring out towards the starry sky.

Naomi shook her head.

'Listen to your sister, Victoria Stitch,' she said. 'Celestine is right.'

Victoria Stitch crossed her arms huffily over her chest.

'How about I go into hiding *temporarily*?' she asked after a few moments' thought. 'Just until we can work out a different plan.'

Celestine nodded. It was better than nothing. And maybe, given a bit of time, she could persuade her sister to change her mind further.

'Tomorrow then,' she said. 'You must go into hiding tomorrow!'

'*After* tomorrow,' said Victoria Stitch. 'Give me one more day in my magnificent palace, at least. We'll be going back down to Naomi's cottage by the sea after that anyway.'

'I don't think so,' said Celestine. 'It's not safe! Salix and Kasper could already be at the museum, waiting for you.'

'But they won't be able to get to me in my palace,' said Victoria Stitch. 'It's surrounded by humans, and there are guards everywhere.'

'But they'll follow you when you leave and find out where you and Naomi live. They'll wait until you're alone, and then they'll kill you!'

Victoria Stitch felt prickles run all the way up and down her arms.

'They won't be able to follow me,' she said. 'We'll be going back to the cottage by car. Too fast for wisklings to follow!'

Celestine shook her head.

'They could slip into the car,' she said.

Victoria Stitch frowned. Suddenly she grabbed Celestine's wrists, hard.

'Listen!' she said, her antennae sparkling with mischief. 'What if Naomi and I don't go back to the cottage after I've been on show in my palace tomorrow? What if we lead Salix and Kasper somewhere else? Set a trap for them in a place where they think they can get to me alone. But you and Tiska could be hiding nearby. We could capture them, and you could bring them back to Wiskling Wood to put in prison for attempted murder. Force them to tell Wiskling Wood what Lord Astrophel's been up to. Expose him!'

'Expose him?!' gasped Celestine. 'I've thought about it but . . . I couldn't! I don't think wisklings would believe me. Do you think they would really believe he was capable of murder?!'

'They would if you told them it was true,' said Victoria Stitch. 'You're *Queen*! I don't think you give yourself enough credit.'

'But then everyone would know what you had done, too,' said Celestine.

'So what!' shrugged Victoria Stitch. 'It's no less than other wisklings expect of me anyway.'

'I don't know . . .' said Celestine.

'It's time wisklings knew the truth about Lord Astrophel,' said Victoria Stitch. 'I think you *should* expose him! Don't let him keep controlling us like this.'

Celestine looked thoughtful. *This* is why she needed her sister. Celestine had thought confronting Lord Astrophel was too dangerous, but maybe her sister was right. Why should Lord Astrophel have the power to control everything in Wiskling Wood like this? *She* was supposed to be the Queen! The one in control. But since taking the throne she'd never felt so restricted. Maybe there *was* something she could do about it.

'We'd have to get Tiska to help,' said Celestine, gazing out of the window just as a fizzle of seaweed green appeared in the distance. 'I'll fly out and talk to her. She'll never come into this hotel room. Never!'

'OK,' said Victoria Stitch, nodding at Naomi to

open the window.

'I'll be back!' said Celestine. 'To tell you the plan. Don't move!' And she whizzed off, leaving a trail of diamond sparks to dissipate in the air.

Victoria Stitch pressed her face against the window, the glitter on her eyelashes sparkling in the silvery moonlight. She saw Celestine's bloom sparks get smaller and smaller until they reached Tiska's green ones in the distance, and then both of them disappeared. For once, for the first time in her life, Victoria Stitch did as she was told and stayed where she was. Eventually, Celestine appeared on the sill again. Victoria Stitch didn't see where she had come from, but she landed right in front of the glass and tapped on it. Naomi slid the window open once more and Celestine stepped inside. Her hair was windswept and she looked breathless and excited.

'Tiska's gone straight back down to the coast!' she said. 'To wait for us back at her hideout. This is the plan. Tomorrow, you can be on display in your palace again. I'm sure Salix and Kasper will be watching you all day through the window—they won't be able to get into the museum; there are so many humans around! At the end of the day, they'll be sure to trail you when you leave the museum, so Naomi will get you straight into a waiting car, leaving the boot open so that Salix and Kasper can slip inside too. We'll drive straight down to the coast and head to the deserted beach where Tiska's hideout is. Naomi will leave you there. Salix and Kasper will think you're alone! But Tiska and Ruby will already be waiting, and I'll be there, too, of course. We'll all ambush Salix and Kasper before they can hurt you!'

Victoria Stitch's eyes glittered.

'We'll have to make sure we leave the boot open for long enough so that the explorers can sneak into it without being seen by humans,' she said. 'Or they'll never keep up with the car, all the way back down to the coast.'

'True,' said Celestine. 'But we can get Naomi to help with that!' She looked up hopefully at the human.

'Will you help?' she asked.

'Of course!' said Naomi.

'Thank you.' Celestine smiled. And then she yawned.

'You're going to have to stay here with me tonight!' said Victoria Stitch, gleefully. 'You can share my doll's house bed!'

CHAPTER 19

'I need to go out with a big, glittering BANG!' said Victoria Stitch to Naomi the following morning. 'If it's to be my last day as a celebrity in the human world.'

While Celestine slept, Victoria Stitch spent a long time getting ready, choosing her favourite dress made by Naomi, with the biggest, puffiest skirt and putting on all the jewellery she had been gifted, until she was dripping with diamonds, opals, and tourmalines. Finally, she placed her biggest star-frosted crown upon her head. It was so big she had to strain to keep her neck upright, but she jutted out her chin, determined to wear it.

'You look . . . *devastating*,' said Naomi.

Victoria Stitch smiled self-assuredly, sticking her foot out from beneath her dress to reveal a shiny, pointed boot done up with violet ribbons. Everything glittered and twinkled.

'I've been thinking,' whispered Victoria Stitch. 'If I disappear for a bit, think how much of an impact it will have when I reappear again. The world will go wild! I'm going to work on a magnificent plan to return.'

Naomi raised her eyebrows, but she didn't say anything as Victoria Stitch stuck her black-tipped wiskling nose in the air, picked up her skirts, and pranced across the sink top towards her bloom.

It wasn't long before Victoria Stitch, Celestine, and Naomi were on their way to the museum. Celestine had been a bit unsure about getting into the handbag at first.

'It's not right!' she'd said as she'd reluctantly slipped into it. 'A wiskling travelling in a human handbag!'

'I find it quite comfortable,' said Victoria Stitch. 'Look, there's a fluffy scarf to sit on, some books to read by wand light, *and* snacks!'

Soon, light came pouring through the slit at the top of the handbag and Naomi's big face loomed down.

'We're here, in the exhibition room,' she whispered.

Victoria Stitch grinned up at Naomi in the diamond light of her wand.

'Look after Celestine today, won't you!' she said.

'Of course,' whispered Naomi. 'Celestine and I will wait nearby, outside the museum. We'll try and spot Salix and Kasper so that we know they definitely *are* watching you. Are you sure you'll be safe without me in your palace?'

'Lord Astrophel's explorers won't be able to get to

me with all the humans around!' said Victoria Stitch confidently. She popped her head out of the bag for a moment, looking round at the great exhibition room and admiring her magnificent palace with a tinge of regret. She hoped it would still be standing when she reappeared again one day. Hopefully soon!

'See you later, Celestine,' she whispered, glancing back down into the depths of the bag where Celestine was sitting, her anxious face aglow with wand light.

'Be careful, Victoria Stitch!' said Celestine.

Victoria Stitch blew dark, cherry-pink kisses to her sister and then jumped out of the handbag and hurried towards the little door at the bottom of the stand, and with Stardust fluttering at her ear, she slipped inside. The staircase rose up in front of her in the gloom. With her wand held out in front of her, she hurried up the stairs, diamond light shuddering on the walls as she bobbed up and down. She was almost at the trapdoor at the top of the staircase, when she bumped into something in front of her. Something that she couldn't see! Fear clutched at her throat as what felt like a gloved hand was pressed over her neck, and someone gripped onto her wrists, holding them behind her back. Her wand fell from her hand, clattering down the stairs.

CHAPTER 20

'Where's the poison, Salix?!' hissed a gruff voice in the darkness. 'Put it against her lips!'

Victoria Stitch was about to scream, but instead, she pressed her lips tightly shut, making a strangled 'mhmhm' sound.

Suddenly, Victoria Stitch felt something hard and cold press right against her mouth. It felt exactly like the top of a bottle. She almost gagged at the strong smell of it.

'Drink!' ordered a different, more high-pitched voice. This wiskling sounded frightened, less sure of himself.

Victoria Stitch tried to shake her head, but she was being held so tightly against the wall by the gruffer-voiced wiskling that there was hardly any room for movement. And now one of them was holding her nose so she couldn't breathe. She was going to have to open her mouth in a minute to get some air and they would pour the poison into her mouth! She was going to die! She wished she still had hold of her wand. Celestine would have no idea what was happening—Salix and Kasper must have found a way to break into her palace overnight. Victoria Stitch felt anger stirring in the pit of her stomach, boiling and bubbling, just as there came a flapping sound, right near her face. Stardust! He beat his wings as fast and hard as he could, knocking the bottle right out of what must have been Salix's hands. Victoria Stitch heard it clatter down the staircase.

'The bottle!' cried the gruff-voiced wiskling. 'Get it Salix! 'I'll hold her! It had better not be spilled.'

Victoria Stitch felt the weaker, shakier grip loosening as Salix let go of her to run down the staircase. With one almighty wrench, she twisted out of Kasper's grip and pelted down the stairs herself, pushing past Salix and tumbling, head over heels, back out of the entrance door, Stardust fluttering behind her. She could just see Naomi and her mum about to head out of the doors of the exhibition room.

'NAOMI!!!' she screeched, and Naomi turned round in surprise.

'What's the matter?' she asked. 'Did you forget something?'

'Yes!' said Victoria Stitch, with a wild look in her eyes.

Naomi hurried over and knelt on the floor.

'They're in there,' whispered Victoria Stitch, pointing towards the door with a shaking fingertip. 'Salix and Kasper! They just tried to kill me!'

Naomi gasped.

'You have to capture them!' said Victoria Stitch. 'They're using the invisibility spell, so you'll have to feel for them. Quick! Put your hand in and catch them. Put them in your handbag! And move Celestine to your pocket!'

Naomi looked about her worriedly, and then rolled up her sleeve and swiftly stuck her hand into the wiskling-sized

passageway.

'Thank you, Naomi, for checking the staircase. I am sure I saw a spider!' cried Victoria Stitch, for the benefit of the puzzled security guards looking on.

'I can't feel anything,' Naomi muttered. And then, 'Ouch! Something's jabbing me!'

'What's going on Naomi?' asked her mum from the other side of the room.

'Nothing!' said Naomi. 'Victoria Stitch thought she saw a spider, that's all. Ooh. Ow!' Naomi winced in pain again but stuck her arm further up the miniature staircase.

'Ah, here it is!' she said, brightly, bringing out her hand. It was closed in a fist, but the squashy skin on her fingers and thumb kept moving and dimpling, as though there was something flailing about in her grip. No one would be able to notice unless they were up close. Suddenly a drop of red blood appeared on her finger, and Naomi gave a little squeal, hurriedly dropping whatever it was into the inner pocket of her handbag and zipping it up. At the same time, she gently scooped up a surprised Celestine and slipped her into her pocket instead.

'Did you get both of the explorers?' hissed Victoria Stitch, hopping up and down, impatiently. Naomi shot her hand back into the entrance, feeling up the staircase as far as she could.

'I think I only have one!' she said. 'And I can't feel anything else up there. He must have already escaped, or else he's hiding in there somewhere.'

'No!' said Victoria Stitch, panic beginning to rise within her.

'Is everything alright?' asked one of the guards, walking over to the palace. 'Is Victoria Stitch ready to go in? There's a big queue waiting outside the door.'

'Oh,' said Naomi, thinking quickly. 'Well, it's just that . . . Victoria Stitch told me she doesn't feel too well today.'

'I don't,' said Victoria Stitch, putting her hand up to her forehead and swooning rather melodramatically. 'I'm suddenly not at all well enough to be on show today.'

'Oh, dear!' said Elizabeth, hurrying over. 'We had better get you back to the hotel then, Victoria Stitch.'

CHAPTER 21

As soon as they were all back at the hotel and Elizabeth was safely in her own room, with the adjoining door closed, Celestine popped her head out of Naomi's pocket. Naomi was staring at Victoria Stitch with a panicked look in her eyes.

'What now?' she asked. 'There's a wiskling in my handbag who wants to kill you! And another one on the loose!'

'We have to make sure he doesn't escape!' said Victoria Stitch. 'We should lock ourselves in the en-suite bathroom and make him wash off the invisibility potion.'

'Wash it off?' asked Naomi.

'Yes,' said Victoria Stitch. 'The invisibility spell is

a forbidden spell from the *Book of Wiskling*. You use your birth-crystal dust and smudge it onto your body in a certain way. It makes you invisible until you wash it off. I'm surprised Lord Astrophel allowed Salix and Kasper to learn a forbidden spell. No one is supposed to know the forbidden spells in the *Book of Wiskling*. No one! He must have been desperate to get rid of me at whatever cost.'

'What *exactly* has happened?' interjected Celestine, a little crossly. Her hair looked rather dishevelled from being so hastily put into Naomi's pocket.

'Salix and Kasper were waiting for me inside MY palace!' said Victoria Stitch. 'They tried to poison me, but I managed to escape. We caught one of them, but the other has fled. They must have snuck in there during the night and were lying in wait for me.'

'But, how on earth did they manage to get in?' frowned Celestine. 'There are so many human guards in the museum.'

'They're under the invisibility spell!' growled Victoria Stitch.

Celestine didn't look as surprised as Victoria Stitch had thought she might. Instead, her face clouded over with fury.

'I've been starting to suspect that Lord Astrophel has been using the *Book of Wiskling* lately,' she said. 'Well, at least we managed to catch one of the explorers. Let's speak to him!'

Victoria Stitch, Celestine, and Naomi hurried across to the en-suite bathroom, and Naomi locked the door firmly behind them.

'Fill the sink with water!' ordered Victoria Stitch. 'And tip him in!'

Naomi ran the taps in the sink. Then, as quick as a flash, she opened the top of the handbag, unzipped the inside pocket, and turned it upside down, shaking it roughly. Notebooks full of fashion drawings, tubes of lip balm, her purse, and the hotel keys all came tumbling out into the water along with something else that made a small splash. Immediately, sparkling green streaks appeared in the water.

'Birth-crystal dust,' said Victoria Stitch. 'It's washing off!'

Gradually, a wiskling began to materialize, his clothes sopping wet. He was tall, with dark hair and eyebrows, and his antennae sparkled green. On his back was a backpack, which his rolled-up leaf and wand stuck out from. He looked terrified as he gazed from Victoria Stitch to Celestine and then up at Naomi.

'A human!' he gasped, and immediately tried to duck down behind some of the detritus in the sink.

'Don't try and hide from us!' said Celestine, suddenly feeling a surge of power rising within her. 'You won't be able to.'

The explorer peeped out from behind a tube of cherry lip balm.

'Queen Celestine!' he stuttered. 'What are you doing here?'

'Never mind that,' said Celestine, quite enjoying feeling like a proper queen for once. 'Give me your leaf and your wand now!'

'But . . .' began the wiskling.

'Hand them over,' said Celestine. 'And any birth-crystal dust you have, too. I don't want you using the invisibility spell again.'

Reluctantly, the explorer handed over his wand—a peridot moon—and dug in his backpack for a small glass jar, which was filled with a sparkling peridot green powder. Naomi took

it, lifting it close to her eyes and marvelling at it.

'Birth-crystal dust?' she said. 'Absolutely fascinating!'

Naomi put the tiny bottle, leaf, and wand into her pocket, while the explorer looked on in dismay. He was trapped and defenceless without them. Celestine put her hands on her hips and stared angrily down at the explorer.

'You're in big trouble!' she said. 'You'll go to prison for attempted murder! Now, which explorer are you? Salix or Kasper?'

'Salix,' stammered the wiskling, and then he burst into tears.

'I'm so sorry, Your Majesty!' he sobbed. 'I didn't want to do it. Lord Astrophel gave me no choice . . . he threatened me with life imprisonment. He said killing Victoria Stitch was for the good of Wiskling Wood. She has revealed herself to humans! She's putting all of Wiskling Wood in danger!'

'But you should never have tried to *murder* her!' said Celestine, feeling another surge of exhilaration from the power she seemed to be wielding over this frightened wiskling. 'Murder is *always* wrong,' she continued. 'Lord Astrophel tried to have my sister murdered. He doesn't deserve his power. We must tell Wiskling Wood the truth!'

'We?' said Salix, his voice shaking.

'Yes,' said Celestine. We're going to need your help, Salix. From now on you work for *us*.'

Salix nodded, his eyes large and fearful.

'Of course, Queen Celestine,' he said. 'Please forgive me. I'm so sorry.' And then he burst into a fresh round of tears.

'Well, you may as well get out and get dry,' said Celestine. Naomi, who had been looking on in astonishment, grabbed a clean, white flannel and helped a very reluctant Salix climb up the slippy side of the sink, before holding it out towards him. He snatched at it warily, before hurrying across the sink top, getting as far away from Naomi as possible.

'It would be better to find Kasper so we can take them both back to the wood,' said Victoria Stitch. 'Salix, do you have any idea where Kasper will be now?'

Salix shook his head, cowering in the corner of the sink top.

'Well, where do you *think* he might have gone?' prodded Victoria Stitch. 'What would *you* have done if Kasper had been the one to be captured?'

'I guess I would follow to see where you took him,' said Salix. 'And as soon as I discovered that Queen Celestine was in the human world, I would go straight home to see Lord Astrophel.'

'Hmm,' said Victoria Stitch. 'If Lord Astrophel knows that Celestine has been in the human world then that puts her in great danger. She knows too much. He'll do all he can to get rid of her, I'm sure! We need to get Celestine back to Wiskling Wood as soon as possible! Ideally before Kasper! She can still go ahead with the plan of exposing him—we have Salix, at least—but the sooner the better! Before Lord Astrophel has time to try and stop her!'

CHAPTER 22

'MUM!' cried Naomi, bursting through the adjoining door between their rooms. 'We need to go back home, right now!'

Elizabeth looked up, frowning,

'Why?' she asked.

'Fairies need sea air to recover from illness!' said Naomi.

'I do!' swooned Victoria Stitch, from where she was perched on Naomi's hand. 'I need it as soon as possible, or I might *die!*'

'Gosh!' said Elizabeth, hurriedly putting down the book that she had been reading. 'Poor Victoria Stitch. We had better leave right away! I'd better call our driver!' She jumped off the bed and began to run around the room, throwing things into her suitcase.

Naomi hurried back through the adjoining door and put Victoria Stitch gently into her handbag on the bed where Celestine was hiding.

Salix was in the hotel wardrobe for the time being.

'I'm not leaving you alone with him in the handbag, even for one minute!' Victoria Stitch had said to Celestine a few moments before. 'He can't get far without his leaf or wand, and we've tied his hands behind his back with dental floss, but even so . . . I don't trust him one bit!'

So, Salix had been put at the back of the hotel wardrobe by Naomi, and there he stayed until they were ready to leave.

_____

Fifteen minutes later, Elizabeth and Naomi—now with all three wisklings secreted in her handbag— checked out of the hotel and hurried out of the back doors to where a black car was waiting for them. Victoria Stitch heard the car doors slam closed and the engine start. They were off!

'Is Victoria Stitch going to stay in the handbag for the whole journey?' she heard Elizabeth say through the muffled walls of patent leather.

'She's sleeping wrapped up in my scarf,' lied Naomi. 'She feels very ill.'

'Poor Victoria Stitch,' said Elizabeth. 'I hope it

wasn't the prawn salad we ate last night. I didn't know fairies could get ill like this.'

'I'm sure she'll be better soon,' said Naomi. 'After some proper rest in her doll's house.'

'Yes,' agreed Elizabeth. 'I shall make her some heartwarming soup.'

Inside the handbag, Victoria Stitch felt a glow of warmth. Elizabeth was the closest thing she'd ever had to a mother. She glanced at Celestine in the diamond light of her wand. Celestine's expression was wistful.

The journey back to the cottage was long and trafficky. There was nothing to do inside the handbag but talk. Victoria Stitch and Celestine both lit their wands so that a diamond glow fell over them all, and Naomi poked snacks in through the opening. Salix sat huddled up in the corner of the bag, but he seemed less afraid after his time in the wardrobe.

'When we get back to Wiskling Wood, you must come with me to do a speech from the palace balcony,' said Celestine. 'Tell everyone the truth about Lord Astrophel, and your prison sentence *may* be reduced.'

Salix nodded as though defeated. Victoria Stitch scowled at him.

'I'm not letting you go back into Wiskling Wood alone with him, Celestine,' she said. 'But there's no way *I* can go back in with you! I'd probably get arrested the second I stepped back through the gate!'

'We'll go and fetch Tiska on the way,' said Celestine. 'I can remember the way to her hideout.'

Victoria Stitch shot Salix a dark glare. He withered under her gaze.

'I won't do anything to harm your sister,' he said. 'I promise I'll do everything Queen Celestine tells me to. Please, I just want all this to be over!'

He hung his head regretfully, his dark eyebrows knotting up. Celestine felt herself thawing towards him, just a tiny bit.

'Do you have a family, Salix?' she asked.

'I have children,' he whispered.

'Oh!' said Celestine, taken aback. Despite the fact that Salix had tried to kill Victoria Stitch, she felt a tinge of remorse that Salix was going to go to prison on her orders. She would be taking a father away from his children. They would grow up without one. Just like her and Victoria Stitch.

'Aquamarine and Tanzanite,' said Salix. 'Those are their birth crystals.'

Celestine glanced at Victoria Stitch, feeling uncomfortable, but Victoria Stitch just looked on suspiciously, blinking her long wiskling eyelashes in the dim light.

'Once I had my children, I started to think it was risky being an explorer, actually,' Salix continued. 'I was about to give it up when Lord Astrophel entrusted me with this mission. I had no choice but to follow his orders! He threatened me with life imprisonment! I considered not doing as he asked and just going into hiding forever in the human world, but then I would never see my children again . . .'

'Oh, my goodness!' said Celestine, and Victoria Stitch gave her a sharp look.

'He could be lying about all this!' she said. 'Stop letting him pull on your heartstrings, Celestine!'

'I don't think he is lying!' said Celestine. 'Look at him! He's completely torn up! And don't worry, he's still going to prison. He tried to *kill* you! But I'm not sure he deserves a life sentence.'

'Humph!' said Victoria Stitch, crossing her arms over her chest.

'I never wanted any part in this!' Salix continued. 'I swear I didn't!'

'What about Kasper?' asked Celestine. 'Did Lord Astrophel force him into it, too?'

Salix shook his head.

'Kasper didn't need forcing into it,' he said. 'Kasper's . . . different from me. He's already done jobs for Lord Astrophel. He's much more ruthless.

Between Kasper and Lord Astrophel my hands were tied. I had no choice but to go along with what they wanted.'

'There's always a choice!' snapped Victoria Stitch.

'Maybe there really wasn't,' said Celestine, and Victoria Stitch gave her an astonished look.

'Celestine . . .' she began.

'No, listen,' said Celestine. 'Lord Astrophel allowed Kasper and Salix to use the invisibility spell. That's a forbidden spell from the *Book of Wiskling*. He had access to the *Book of Wiskling*, Victoria Stitch! And I think he's been using it a lot lately to control me and everything that happens in the wood. It all makes sense to me now! That's why I feel like I can never stand up to him. That's why I feel so trapped!'

Salix began to nod vigorously.

'I think he must have used some persuasion magic on me, too!' he said.

'I wouldn't put it past him,' said Celestine, frowning. 'We're going to have to be really careful when we go back into the wood. Lord Astrophel is dangerous.'

It was early evening when the car finally crunched down the lane in front of the cottage. It was quiet and still. Naomi and Elizabeth got out of the car and waved the driver away. As soon as Elizabeth had gone inside the house, Victoria Stitch and Celestine shot out of Naomi's handbag on their blooms in a flurry of gold and silver sparks.

'We have to get Celestine to the entrance of Wiskling Wood!' said Victoria Stitch. 'As fast as possible! I know the way from here by bloom! It's not far.'

'OK!' said Naomi, excitedly. 'Let me come with you. I can ride my bike to keep up!'

'Oh, no!' said Victoria Stitch shaking her head, and she immediately flew down and alighted on Naomi's shoulder.

'I'm sorry,' she said. 'I trust you with my whole heart, but I can never show you where the entrance to Wiskling Wood is. Some things are just sacred.'

'Oh,' said Naomi, her face falling. 'OK. I understand.' She glanced down at the handbag.

'What about Salix?' she asked. 'Is he going with you?

'No,' said Victoria Stitch, suddenly. I don't trust him to go back into the wood with Celestine.

'I thought he was supposed to come?' said Celestine. 'He's going to help me expose Lord Astrophel! And we're going to fetch Tiska on the way. That was the plan. I think we *can* trust him Victoria Stitch.'

'I've changed my mind,' said Victoria Stitch.

'I'm not sure you need him there. Wisklings will believe you! You're Queen! It's safer if Naomi keeps him captive for now, and you can send out some guards to collect him later if we leave him in a remote spot. I don't like the idea of him going into the wood with you, even if Tiska is there.'

'You *can* trust me,' said Salix, popping his head over the top of the bag. 'I swear to you! Please let me go back into the wood. I just want to see my children again!'

'Let him come,' said Celestine. 'I'll be safe with Tiska. Salix, you can come!'

Victoria Stitch arched her eyebrows.

'On your own crown be it, Celestine,' she snapped. 'I won't be there to protect you once you're in the wood. Give him his leaf so he can fly with us, Naomi. But not his wand, or crystal dust! Let me untie his hands. I'm going to use the string to tether him to Celestine's bloom.'

'Right,' said Naomi, reaching into her pocket and bringing out Salix's leaf, which was now a little crumpled. Victoria Stitch immediately swooped down and snatched it out of her hand. Then she flew over to the handbag from which Salix was peering out.

'I hope we *can* trust you,' she said. 'If not, just

remember: *I* know who you are. And if you harm my sister I will come back into Wiskling Wood and *destroy* your life!'

'I won't!' said Salix, earnestly. 'I swear!'

'Come on!' said Celestine 'We have to go! There's still a chance we can get back to the wood before Kasper!'

Victoria Stitch untied Salix's hands and used the string to tether his leaf to Celestine's bloom. Then she hovered behind them both in the air, holding her wand out in front of her.

'One wrong move, Salix,' she warned, 'and I'll blast you with the sleeping spell.'

Salix gulped as he glanced down from where they were all hovering in the air above Naomi's head. It was a long way down.

'You look like three little fireworks!' said Naomi, as she gazed up at them in the low light.

'You *will* be back . . . won't you, Victoria Stitch?' she asked anxiously.

'Of course!' said Victoria Stitch. 'I'd never leave you, Naomi. You're my best friend! *I'm* not going into Wiskling Wood! When Celestine tells them what I've been up to, I'll be hated even more than I already am!'

'Well, I'm glad this isn't the last time I'm going

to see you!' said Naomi, breathing a sigh of relief. 'I don't know what I'd do without you, Victoria Stitch. You've just made mine and Mum's life so much better ever since you appeared! You're just *magic!*'

Victoria Stitch beamed down at Naomi. It was one of the nicest things anyone had ever said to her.

'You'll never know how much you've helped *me,*' she replied. 'Don't worry, Naomi. I'll be back!' She blew cherry-pink kisses in the air and then whizzed upwards towards the milky stars.

From up in the sky, Victoria Stitch could see the beaches down below. There was the one that was nearest to Naomi's house, and then there were some more further along, including the one where Tiska's hideout was. They started to head in that direction, Victoria Stitch flying right behind Salix the whole time, pointing her wand at his back. Before they even landed on Tiska and Ruby's beach, a fizzle of seaweed green and a sparkle of red shot up into the sky.

'Celestine!' cried Tiska, her emerald hair streaming out behind her. 'What's happened? We've been watching and waiting and then spotted your sparks in the sky. This wasn't the plan!' She jerked her thumb at Salix. 'Who's this?'

'The plan has changed!' said Celestine. 'I'll explain on the way. We need to get back to Wiskling Wood as fast as possible. Will you and Ruby come?'

'Of course!' said Tiska.

Victoria Stitch breathed a sigh of relief. Celestine would be protected by both Tiska *and* Ruby! She had never felt so pleased to see her sister's best friend!

The five wisklings continued to fly along the coast until they reached the beach they needed to get to. It had a stream of water running down the centre of it that fed into the sea. If they followed the stream inland, it would lead them through some open fields before disappearing into a wood, where the entrance to Wiskling Wood was. Victoria Stitch felt a fluttering start up inside her as they changed direction, following the silver ribbon of water upstream. She hadn't been anywhere near Wiskling Wood since coming to the human world. But she wanted to make sure Celestine got back safely. The whole time, she flew right behind Salix, keeping her wand pointed right at his back.

They reached the wood and flew into the trees, still following the ribbon of water upstream.

'We have to find the tree with the star carved into it,' said Celestine. 'It's somewhere on the left-hand side.'

'I know exactly where the entrance is,' said Tiska. 'I'm an explorer, remember!' She whizzed up in front

of them all, gesturing for them to follow.

Victoria Stitch and Celestine followed Tiska's green, sparkly trail as she flew confidently up the stream. The sparks reflected on the surface of the burbling water, making it glitter.

'Here!' said Tiska suddenly, stopping by a large tree right next to the stream. She swooped low, pointing at a small star that had been carved into the trunk. Parallel to it was a hazy patch of air that faintly sparkled. As soon as they all landed, Victoria Stitch immediately grabbed onto Salix's arm.

'Don't even think of going through without Celestine!' she hissed.

'I wasn't going to!' said Salix. 'But you'd better hide, Victoria Stitch. Before someone sees you through the magic.'

Victoria Stitch scooted round the trunk of the tree, beckoning to Celestine to follow her, while Tiska and Ruby took over holding both Salix's arms tight.

'Are you sure about this?' Victoria Stitch asked. 'I'm starting to get scared about you going back in. What if wisklings side with Lord Astrophel? What will everyone think about what I've done?!'

'I've got Tiska and Ruby with me,' said Celestine. 'And Salix. There's three of us against him. And besides, as soon as the guard at the gate sees me, he'll protect me too! I'll ask him to accompany us back to the palace. I don't think Lord Astrophel will have a chance to get close. And anyway, Kasper might not have even got back to Wiskling Wood yet. Lord Astrophel could still be unaware I'm even in the human world! I'm going to go straight to the palace to make a speech from the balcony. I'm going to expose Lord Astrophel before he has time to stop me! And if wisklings side with him then well . . . I'll come back into the human world and go into hiding with you.'

'I would actually love that!' said Victoria Stitch, wickedly. Then she grabbed Celestine and pulled her into a hug so fierce that Celestine thought her bones might break.

'I'm sorry I've made things difficult for you,' she said. 'Do you think the wisklings will be happy to just let me stay in the human world?'

'I don't know,' said Celestine. 'I don't know *what* everyone will think. Maybe they won't agree. Some might take the law into their own hands. So it's important you stay in hiding so no wisklings can find you! You have to stay in hiding, Victoria Stitch. I can't protect you from inside the wood!'

'I'll stay at Naomi's,' said Victoria Stitch. 'Maybe you can come and visit me there sometimes? In secret!'

'Of course!' said Celestine. 'I'll find a way.'

'OK,' smiled Victoria Stitch, but she was holding back tears. The thought of Celestine disappearing back to a place where she could never go was almost unbearable.

'I hope you manage to bring Lord Astrophel down,' she said. 'I wish I could come back in with you to watch it all!'

'I wish you could too,' said Celestine. 'Do you really think it would be that bad if you came back to Wiskling Wood?'

Victoria Stitch stared at her twin, aghast.

'I could never come back to Wiskling Wood!' she said. 'I don't belong there. Everyone hates me. And besides, I've broken wiskling law. I would be thrown into prison.'

Celestine nodded, but her eyes were full of tears.

'I wish you could stay by my side,' she said. 'I wish . . .'

'Celestine!' came Tiska's voice. 'We have to go!'

Celestine let go of Victoria Stitch. She watched her sister hurry back towards Salix and Tiska. Victoria Stitch looked at Salix, his antennae sputtering green sparks, and narrowed her eyes.

CHAPTER 23

CELESTINE stood with Tiska, Ruby, and Salix in front of the hazy, faintly sparkling patch of air.

'We just have to step through,' said Tiska, 'and we'll arrive at the entrance to Wiskling Wood, right up at the top of the stream in the north. There's a sort of holding area in front of the gate.'

As soon as Celestine put her foot through the shimmering haze and stepped down onto the ground on the other side, she could see two golden gates up ahead, much like the ones at the exit. One gate sunk down into the water for boats to pass through and the other was on the bank, next to an office. There was a scruffy-haired guard sitting outside on a chair.

'Queen Celestine!' he said, jumping up. 'Your Majesty! What are you doing here?'

'I had business to attend to,' said Celestine, trying to sound as authoritative as possible. 'Please let us through, on royal orders! And then I would be most grateful if you would accompany us back to the palace?'

The guard dithered for a moment, his bushy orange eyebrows knotting and unknotting. He was tall and strong-looking with a rough sort of face. He would make the perfect protection to the palace, Celestine thought.

Eventually, the guard took the key from his belt, asking no more questions.

'You may go through, Your Majesty,' he said. 'And of course I will accompany your party back to the palace.'

'Who will guard the gate while you are gone?' asked Tiska.

'It will just have to stay locked and unmanned for a few hours,' said the guard. 'Any wisklings wanting to come back in will have to wait.'

Celestine was glad of the guard's protection as the four of them flew south, back towards Spellbrooke and the palace. She had made it back to Wiskling Wood safely! Now she just had to get to the palace and out onto the balcony to do a speech without coming into contact with Lord Astrophel. They flew high up in the air, keeping away from other wisklings who were out on their blooms and leaves, and Celestine kept her hood pulled down low over her face, though she didn't feel too worried about being spotted. She and Victoria Stitch had switched blooms back at the hotel and she was riding her old buttercup. It felt familiar, like an old friend. No one would recognize it as the Queen's bloom.

It seemed busy in the sky tonight, and as they flew south, downstream towards the more populated areas, they saw more and more wisklings out and about. More than usual, Celestine thought. There was a strange feeling in the air. An excited fizzing. It made her feel anxious.

'Has something happened in Wiskling Wood?' Celestine asked, calling out to the guard in front.

'Not that I know of!' said the guard. 'But I'll admit, there *is* a strange atmosphere afoot tonight.'

It was completely dark by the time they reached the palace, and Celestine's hands were aching from holding onto the stalk of her bloom for so long. The streetlamps were all alight, glow crystals shining out from within their petals, flickering purple, pink, and orange. The parade in front of the palace was awash with wisklings, scurrying about and chattering in excited groups. Celestine frowned, landing at the back gates of the palace with a skid, pleased to see that both Art and Blue were on duty. Tiska and Ruby immediately grabbed on tightly to Salix's arms.

'Your Majesty!' gasped Art. 'I thought you'd come back early from Twila's when you heard the news. Congratulations!'

'What news are you talking about?' asked Celestine, her heart beginning to race in her chest. Tell me!'

A quizzical expression passed across Art's face.

'How have you not heard?' he asked. 'The news came out this morning! A new diamond baby has appeared on the wall of the Crystal Cave!'

CHAPTER 24

CELESTINE clutched onto Tiska for support, feeling dizzy. A new diamond baby! Destined to become royalty and rule Wiskling Wood one day. When it was born it would be sent to the palace to be brought up as a prince or princess. And as the current diamond royal in charge, it would be up to *Celestine* to raise it!

'That's . . . wonderful news,' she managed to say, after a moment. She took a few deep breaths. This was big. Really big! But she mustn't get distracted. She had other things to do first. Terrifying, overwhelming things. She had no idea how wisklings would react to her speech exposing Lord Astrophel. But she had no choice but to do it now. It wouldn't be long before he knew that she'd been in the human world, and once he knew that, she would be in great danger.

'Art, please spread the word that I will shortly be giving a speech on my balcony, and I would like as many wisklings in attendance as possible.'

Art nodded, then he opened the gate to let Celestine, Tiska, Ruby, and Salix through. Celestine turned to wave at the scruffy-haired guard who had escorted them all the way from the entrance gate, but he had already gone.

Celestine hurried up the path through the palace gardens and the back doors, where she was detained by more guards congratulating her on the news of the diamond baby.

'Thank you,' she replied, feeling flustered. 'I'm going straight up to my balcony to do a speech. 'Do not let anyone else into the palace, do you understand?'

'Of course,' said the guards, frowning wonderingly but not daring to ask questions under the unusually commanding tone of the Queen. They nodded and stepped aside respectfully.

Celestine scooted inside the palace and into the grand entrance hall, realizing she felt more authoritative than usual. Having some time apart from Lord Astrophel had been good for her.

Now Celestine was alone with her friends and Salix

at last! Her antennae fizzed with tiny, golden sparks of nervous energy. And though she was trying to focus on the job at hand, thoughts of the diamond baby growing on the wall of the crystal cave kept creeping into her head. She needed to be there for it when it was born. The idea of Lord Astrophel having any control over it gave her chills. She had to expose him as soon as possible. She knew that he would easily be able to get into the palace if he wanted to. Even though she had told the guards to let no one in. He had the *Book of Wiskling*! What if he was already somehow on his way? Intent on stopping her from using her voice or worse . . . get rid of her. If that happened, then he would have full control over the baby when it was born. It didn't bear thinking about!

'Let's go straight up to the balcony,' Celestine said. 'There are already wisklings on the parade. I saw loads of them. I'll start my speech exposing Lord Astrophel as soon as possible. I'll tell everyone that he planned to murder my sister and that he's been using the forbidden *Book of Wiskling* to control me! The news will spread across the wood like wildfire! Once wisklings know, there'll be nothing he can do!'

'OK!' nodded Tiska, but Salix seemed twitchy. He kept looking around the room, glancing towards the doors.

Celestine turned to Salix as they hurried up the wide crystal staircase. 'I know it will be hard telling everyone the truth about the part you played in this,' she said. 'But having you there will help wisklings believe that Lord Astrophel cannot be trusted. If you're completely honest, I'll make sure your prison sentence is greatly reduced. I'll make sure you can see your children.'

'Yes, Your Majesty,' said Salix.

Celestine pushed open the door to the balcony room and stepped inside, followed by Tiska, Ruby, and Salix. She waved her wand to turn on the lights and firmly closed the door behind her. It was a large, empty room, save for a handful of twirly, leaf-backed chairs that had been arranged in rows in front of tall glass windows that led out to the balcony. Right now, the windows were obscured by heavy gold curtains.

'Come,' said Celestine, beckoning for Tiska, Ruby, and Salix to follow her across the room. Her antennea were sparkling madly and she was shaking all over. Only three more steps and she would be in front of the curtains, ready to open the tall glass windows and step out onto the balcony, where everyone on the parade would immediately see her. She would have to take a voice-magnifying spell, of course. There was a jar full of them by the windows—little sweets infused with her own diamond dust. When she told the waiting crowd what Lord Astrophel had done, would they side with her, or would he still be able to twist her words in some way? Would everyone hate her because of what Victoria Stitch had done? Would Wiskling Wood even still want her to be Queen—especially now there was a new diamond baby on the way? She had no way of knowing. There was a lot to lose if this went wrong.

But also a lot to gain if it goes right, she told herself inside her head. *I have to try! For the sake of the wood, and for the new diamond baby.*

Celestine was just reaching for the heavy gold curtain when there was a clicking sound from behind her. She whirled round to see the door to the balcony room opening. She felt Salix jump next to her as though he had been shot.

A wiskling pushed open the door. Celestine gasped in horror and her blood ran cold.

It was Lord Astrophel.

CHAPTER 25

'MAY I have a word?' said Lord Astrophel, sidling into the room.

Celestine smiled at him, tightly. Her heart was absolutely pounding in her chest and she was aware of Salix standing next to her. Whether Kasper was back in the wood or not, Lord Astrophel must now be aware that she knew everything.

'How did you know I was back?' she asked.

Lord Astrophel smiled, and the scruffy-haired guard from the gate appeared, closing the door behind him. Celestine frowned, confused.

208

'Kasper!' said Salix. 'I was worried you wouldn't get here in time.'

Kasper grinned and his rough face twisted into something quite ugly.

Celestine stared at Salix, horrified.

'But . . .' she said. 'He's the gatekeeper!'

'The gatekeeper is lying on the ground, tied up behind the office,' Kasper sniggered. 'You lot thought you were so clever, but I was a step ahead of you the whole time. Once you captured Salix, I followed you and waited for a chance to get him alone. We had a little chat inside the wardrobe back at the hotel and made a new plan. We knew by then that Celestine planned on coming straight back to Wiskling Wood to expose Lord Astrophel, so I made sure I got back to Wiskling Wood first, to take the guard's place and wait for her. Salix's job was to find out where Victoria Stitch lived with the human.'

'A clever trick,' smirked Lord Astrophel. 'Salix and Kasper will deny all knowledge of their mission, and thanks to you keeping Salix so close, I know Victoria Stitch's exact location. You won't be able to save her this time . . .'

'I'll go out on this balcony right now and tell the truth!' cried Celestine. 'Even without Salix, the wisklings will believe me. They trust me!'

'You won't make it to the balcony because I am going to finish you once and for all,' snarled Lord Astrophel. 'And then I will deal with Victoria Stitch.'

Tears sprang to Celestine's eyes. 'No!'

'I'm afraid so,' said Lord Astrophel.

Celestine glared at Salix.

'You traitor!' she shouted. 'I believed you! You said you had *children!*'

Salix hung his head.

'I'm sorry, Queen Celestine,' he said. 'I really am. I *was* going to do as you asked, but then Kasper turned up while I was in the wardrobe and we made a new plan. I *do* have children. That's why I can't go to prison. They need me! You were going to put me in prison whether I told the truth or not. But Lord Astrophel has promised me freedom!'

Lord Astrophel took a step towards Celestine, and she instinctively took a step back, reaching out for Tiska's hand and squeezing it. What should she do? She knew there were no guards stationed outside the room, and her screams would never be heard over the sound of the crowds outside. She glanced at the gold curtains. Maybe the surest thing to do would be to rip them open, then everyone outside on the parade would be able to see in through the tall glass windows. Lord Astrophel wouldn't be able to do anything in full view of a crowd. She lurched towards the curtains just as Salix lunged towards her. He grabbed her before she could open them, holding tight. Celestine tried to scream, but he put a hand over her mouth.

'Celestine!' cried Tiska, and she and Ruby immediately leapt on Salix, trying to pull him off.

'Wiskimmobiliza!' said Lord Astrophel, calmly, and he twitched his wand towards Tiska, shooting sapphire-blue sparks right into her chest. Tiska flopped down onto the floor with a thump, only her eyes still able to move.

'No!' yelled Ruby, letting go of Salix and sinking down to help Tiska, just as Lord Astrophel sent a stream of sparks towards her, too. She flopped to the floor, paralyzed. Celestine stared in utter horror at her friends and kicked wildly at Salix, but he was surprisingly stronger than he looked.

'If you don't stop flailing,' said Lord Astrophel, 'I'll put the same spell on you. Now do you promise you'll be quiet?'

Celestine glowered at Lord Astrophel, but she stopped struggling, and Salix took his hand off her mouth.

'You're corrupt!' she spat. 'You abuse your power! That's a forbidden spell from the *Book of Wiskling!* No one's supposed to use that kind of dark magic!'

Lord Astrophel shrugged. 'I know a lot more spells than just that one. I won't hesitate to use them.'

'You're loathsome,' hissed Celestine. 'And so are you, Salix and Kasper.'

Kasper grinned evilly, but Salix had the grace to look a little ashamed. Lord Astrophel had a determined look on his face.

'It's all for the good of Wiskling Wood,' he said. 'We wouldn't be in this unfortunate position if you and your sister had followed my rules. But you have both been trouble, ever since the day you were born from that . . . impure crystal.'

He said the word, 'impure', as though he was wiping something nasty off the bottom of his shoe.

'Still, there's a new diamond baby growing on the wall of the crystal cave now,' he said. 'At last! A pure one this time, I hope. He or she will be crowned at birth and I shall use the short time I have left to mould them into the leader this wood needs.'

Celestine stared at Lord Astrophel, aghast. If she died, the diamond baby would grow up under his care. The idea was unbearable. She *had* to try and stop him. But how? She was going to need all her wits about her if she was going to get out of this alive.

'Lord Astrophel!' she begged. 'Do you really want a murder on your hands? Two murders! You know I'm a good queen! Wisklings like me! I swear I won't tell *anyone* about this. And Victoria Stitch has agreed to go into hiding, forever this time. We could just bury this whole thing! It would be much simpler.'

Lord Astrophel's lips twitched into an amused smile.

'It's too late,' he said. 'The damage is done and I don't trust Victoria Stitch or you after your little escapade into the human world. It's time I got what I've always strived for—a harmonious and happy wood. I've come to realize that that's never going to happen while you two are still alive!'

He lifted his wand up in the air again and Celestine flinched. It was a magnificent, sparkling, sapphire moon.

'Wh . . . What are you going to do?' whispered Celestine, and terror began to claw at her throat. She looked down at Tiska and Ruby, who were still lying helpless on the floor. She knew Lord Astrophel would probably 'dispose' of them too.

'I'm going to make this quick and clean,' said Lord Astrophel. 'Hopefully, you'll hardly feel a thing. But I'm not sure how painful the death hex is. I've never experienced it before.'

The death hex. Another spell from the *Book of Wiskling*. The *ultimate* spell from the *Book of Wiskling*.

Celestine hung her head, defeated. She was trapped and now she was going to die.

Lord Astrophel raised his wand in the air.

'Any last words?' he asked.

Celestine raised her head and narrowed her eyes.

'You are a corrupt, conniving, evil wiskling!' she hissed.

Lord Astrophel nodded.

'That's fair, I suppose,' he said. Then he raised his wand higher, pointing it at Celestine. The sapphire moon sparkled under the magnificent chandelier that hung down from the ceiling. Lord Astrophel started to mutter a chilling incantation and Celestine stared back at him, aghast, as blue sparks began to fizz from the end of his wand. She really was going to die! She thought of Victoria Stitch and she thought of the diamond baby, an innocent in all this. It was too much to bear.

Lord Astrophel muttered the last syllable of the spell, when there was an almighty shattering of glass and a dark shape came smashing into the room through the tall glass window, billowing the curtains open, and sending shards of glass flying everywhere.

CHAPTER 26

THE dark figure crashed into Lord Astrophel, and his wand hand swerved in the air, the stream of blue sparks diverting away from Celestine and hitting Salix instead, who let out a strangled cry and fell to the ground. Acrid smoke hissed from his body, and Celestine could hear screams coming from the crowd down below on the parade, who could see everything that was going on through the now open curtains.

Victoria Stitch, for that's who the dark figure was, wheeled round in the air as more deadly sparks came her way, dodging behind the chandelier as another death hex hit. The chandelier exploded into crystal shards, sending sharp fragments flying round the room. Victoria Stitch ducked behind her cape, holding

it up to shield her face as splinters of sharp crystal hit
her legs, drawing blue, wiskling blood.

No longer held by Salix, Celestine leapt to her feet as Lord Astrophel raised his wand once more and pointed it at Victoria Stitch.

'YOU!' he snarled.

'Wiskisomniosa!' screamed Celestine, jabbing her wand in the air. Diamond sparks flurried across the room towards Lord Astrophel, and he looked surprised for a brief moment that she should know such a spell, before he sank to the ground, asleep.

'And *you!*' shouted Celestine, breathlessly, pointing her wand at Kasper who was running for the door. She felt exhilarated as she blasted diamond sparks towards him, too, aware that hundreds of wisklings were watching from the parade. She had never felt so powerful in all her life! Kasper fell to the floor with a thump, just as two palace guards leaf-surfed into the room through the broken palace window.

'There's the intruder!' shouted Art, pointing at Victoria Stitch. He and Blue pelted towards her, grabbing her by the arms and bringing her down to the floor, snatching away her wand and gripping onto her tightly.

'Wait!' cried Celestine. 'Let her go! She's my *sister!* She *saved* me!'

'*Victoria Stitch!?*' Art looked properly at the cloaked figure for a moment and his face took on an expression of astonishment.

'But . . .' he said, 'we saw her break into the palace!'

'LET HER GO!' shouted Celestine again, angrily. 'ON ROYAL ORDERS!'

Art and Blue released their grip on Victoria Stitch and she smoothed down her cloak, haughtily.

'Lord Astrophel was about to kill me with the death hex,' said Celestine. 'He immobilized my friends. Look at them!'

Art and Blue turned to see Tiska and Ruby lying stone still on the floor, while their eyes flicked about wildly.

'And everyone on the parade saw what happened,' said Celestine, gesturing to the window. 'Salix was holding me captive, just as Victoria Stitch burst in and diverted Lord Astrophel from hitting me with the death hex! It's Lord Astrophel and that explorer, there—Kasper—you need to arrest. If it wasn't for Victoria Stitch, I would be dead!!'

Victoria Stitch didn't say anything. She was busy picking the shards of crystal out of her legs, wincing in pain as she did so. Blue blood seeped through her striped tights.

'You need the magics,' said Celestine. 'They'll be able to give you a balm for the cuts.'

'No, I don't!' insisted Victoria Stitch. 'I'm fine!'

But still her eyes watered as she picked at the shards. 'You should comfort Tiska and Ruby, don't worry about me.'

Celestine turned her attention to her friends, kneeling down and taking both their hands.

'It will be OK,' she said. 'We'll find a way to undo this spell, and you can go back to the sea. I know you love it there.'

Tiska's antennae fizzled faintly with emerald sparks.

'The spell will wear off,' Victoria Stitch interjected. 'It's similar to the sleeping spell.'

Art and Blue both looked quizzically at Victoria Stitch.

'Erm . . . so I hear, anyway,' Victoria Stitch said, lowering her head and blinking her long sooty eyelashes fast.

Celestine gazed at her sister in disbelief.

'I can't believe you're here!' she said. 'I thought . . .'

'As soon as you left, I regretted leaving you to go back alone,' said Victoria Stitch. 'I didn't trust *Salix* one bit! And I was right! I knew something was wrong as soon as I stepped up to the gate. Where was the guard? So I had a look around and found the real guard lying behind the office, tied up and gagged. He told me Kasper had tied him up and that you were in danger, so he let me through the gate with a spare key and I flew here as fast as I could!'

'I'm so glad you did!' said Celestine, and she fell on her twin, enveloping her in a huge, tight hug. Their embrace was interrupted by an explosion of activity, as more palace guards burst in, along with the Spellbrooke police in their leaf-green uniforms and boots the colour of red, autumn berries. Celestine told them all once again about how Lord Astrophel had tried to murder her and that Victoria Stitch had saved her life. The police looked at Victoria Stitch with suspicion and Celestine held on tightly to her hand.

Twenty minutes or so later, Tiska and Ruby were able to fully move again and Celestine breathed a sigh of relief. Lord Astrophel and Kasper also came round and found themselves detained, their wrists shackled with handcuffs. So many wisklings outside had witnessed what had happened that there was no choice for them but to tell the truth.

Lord Astrophel stared at Victoria Stitch with poison in his eyes as he was led away by the police.

'None of this would have happened if you hadn't broken one of the most sacred wiskling laws,' he hissed over his shoulder. 'All I've ever done is try to protect the wood. I wish you two had never been *born!*'

Celestine gasped, but Victoria Stitch just raised an eyebrow.

'Enjoy the rest of your life in prison,' she said.

'Oh, you'll be joining me there soon enough!' shouted Lord Astrophel, as he disappeared through the door. 'Once the rest of Wiskling Wood find out what you've *done!* Famous in the human world! Never in all my days . . .'

The guards and police wisklings started to close in around Celestine and Victoria Stitch. There was a frisson of fear in the room.

'Is it true that Victoria Stitch is famous in the human world?' they asked.

'Did she really break the most sacred wiskling law and reveal herself?'

'What's been going on?'

Victoria Stitch didn't say anything. She just hung her head, looking down at the floor while Celestine held on tightly to her arm, an idea beginning to form in her mind. Outside she could hear a low rumbling from the crowd. Even more wisklings had gathered now. They were getting impatient. Demanding to know what had been going on.

'Wiskling Wood deserves to know the truth,' Celestine said, decisively. 'I will make my speech!'

CHAPTER 27

CELESTINE crunched over broken glass and shards of crystal towards the tall windows which led out onto the balcony. It was well after midnight by now, but the crowd on the parade had only grown bigger, illuminated by hundreds of multicoloured spots of wand light. Celestine took one of the voice-magnifying spells from the jar and turned back to Victoria Stitch.

'You won't leave while I'm giving my speech?' she asked.

'Ha!' said Victoria Stitch, darkly, gesturing at all the guards in the room. 'I couldn't even if I tried!'

Celestine popped the voice-magnifying spell into her mouth. Art stood on one side of her and Blue on

the other.

She stepped onto the balcony.

There was silence. Celestine could sense the fear and confusion emanating off the crowd in the darkness. She forced herself to smile and then opened her mouth to speak.

'I know you were all expecting a very different kind of speech tonight,' she began. 'But I have something more important to share with you because I believe you deserve to know the whole truth.'

Celestine could hear confused mutterings from the crowd. She pressed on.

'You all know that four months ago Victoria Stitch escaped the confines of the palace, and we all suspected she had escaped to the human world. I sent my trusted friend Tiska to find her and she returned with news: Victoria Stitch had broken our most sacred wiskling law and showed herself to humans. She is famous there.'

There was a huge gasp among the crowd. Celestine waited a few moments for everyone to calm down.

'I know it's bad,' she said. 'Really bad. It was a stupid and dangerous thing for Victoria Stitch to do. She pretended she was a different sort of creature called a fairy and kept the location of Wiskling Wood a secret. And now—she's back.'

The reaction was mixed. Half of the crowd exploded into fearful shrieks, antennae fizzing like fireworks.

'Arrest her! Put her in prison!' they shouted.

But there were other wisklings, nearer the front of the crowd, who had witnessed Victoria Stitch smash through the window and save their queen from Lord Astrophel.

'*Listen* to the Queen!' they said.

Celestine took a deep breath.

'I know we're all afraid of humans,' she said. 'And while it is true that our world is definitely safer being kept a secret from them, I want you to know that not *all* humans are bad. Some are kind and creative and thoughtful. There is one, in particular, I will always be thankful to for protecting my sister. Without her, I may not be standing here alive right now. Please all raise your wands to Naomi.'

The crowd rippled as hundreds of lit wands were raised tentatively towards the sky, the multicoloured glow from so many different birth crystals twinkling in the darkness.

'Naomi!' shouted Celestine.

'Naomi,' whispered the crowd, uncertainly.

'And for Tiska, too!' said Celestine. 'Brave, kind Tiska! And Ruby!'

This time the crowd roared.

'TISKA! RUBY!'

'And now Victoria Stitch,' said Celestine. 'I know my sister has not always been the most liked wiskling in the wood. And, yes, I agree, some of it is her own doing. But she has been branded as born from an impure crystal at birth and made to feel like she doesn't belong. She felt she had no choice other than to leave the wood and start a life elsewhere. My sister is fierce and my sister is brave. And in the human world, she was free at last. She could be herself, the way no one allowed her to be in Wiskling Wood. Victoria Stitch is not the villain you think she is. Tonight, she risked her life to save mine and to save Wiskling Wood from Lord Astrophel. He's not who you think he is either! He went behind my back and arranged for two explorers to go out into the human world and kill my sister. When I found out what his plans were, he tried to kill me too. With a forbidden spell. Lord Astrophel has the *Book of Wiskling*, and he's been using it to control me.'

The crowd rippled with horror and disgust.

'I know some of you may not agree with what I am about to do,' said Celestine. 'But I refuse to allow any wiskling to make decisions for me, ever again. I am going to issue Victoria Stitch a Royal pardon.' Then she turned and marched back into the room behind the balcony, to where Victoria Stitch sat, clutching Stardust to her chest as though hugging him would make her disappear. Her expression was aghast.

'What are you *doing*?' she hissed. 'I can't believe you, Celestine. I said I'd wait for you to finish your speech, but I am NOT going out on that balcony . . .'

But Celestine grabbed her sister's wrist and pulled, nodding at Art and Blue to help her.

'No!' struggled Victoria Stitch. 'I don't want . . .'

But then she found herself standing in front of the tall windows, looking down at the dark crowd of silent wisklings, the multicoloured glow from their wands mirroring the multicoloured stars in the sky. It was more terrifying than being seen by any human. She felt completely exposed.

Celestine noticed a collective look of terror among the crowd. After all, Victoria Stitch had not been popular before she'd left the wood.

'I can see you're all scared,' said Celestine, still gripping onto Victoria Stitch's wrist hard. 'But this is what you're scared of?' She gestured to Victoria Stitch, with her dishevelled hair and bloodied legs, who uncharacteristically shrunk back from the limelight.

'I don't want to be here, Celestine,' she said,

227

furiously. 'Let me go. I don't belong.'

'Of course, you belong!' boomed out Celestine. 'You're a wiskling. A diamond wiskling, no less. And you just saved me from being murdered and the whole of Wiskling Wood from being under the sneaky dictatorship of a corrupt wiskling. You should be Queen of this wood, alongside me. I don't want another advisor. I want my sister by my side. Wiskling Wood will have two queens. If Lord Astrophel has the power to crown me then I have the power to crown you.'

Victoria Stitch stared at Celestine, horrified.

'Two queens?' muttered the crowd, shocked.

'Victoria Stitch is the moonlight to my sunshine,' said Celestine. 'We were born of the same royal diamond. Wiskling Wood needs both the light and the dark to rule the whole. I know this proposition might seem crazy right now, but this isn't Victoria Stitch's idea, it's mine. Victoria Stitch wants to go back to the human world. Would you prefer the uncertainty of that?'

'No!' shouted a wiskling from the crowd.

'Put her in prison!' someone shouted. 'She broke a sacred wiskling law!'

'No!' boomed Celestine. 'I won't put my sister in prison.'

'Hypocrite,' she heard the wiskling shout. But there were other wisklings, *more* wisklings, who were shouting, too. 'Queen Celestine! Queen Victoria Stitch!'

'Victoria Stitch will be crowned,' Celestine announced. 'And, in time, you will see that it was the right thing to do.'

Victoria Stitch glowered at Celestine, horrified to discover that her eyes were prickling with tears. They began to overflow and run down her face.

Celestine dragged her sister to the front of the balcony.

'You're already wearing a crown!' she joked, but Victoria Stitch just glowered back at her.

'You'll pay for this later,' she hissed. 'They don't really want me; they just feel safer with me here, rather than in the human world.'

'Some of them, maybe,' said Celestine. 'But this is the right thing to do. I feel it in my bones! And you have a chance to prove yourself to them. Show them you can be a good queen. *We* can be good queens, ruling together, making sure Wiskling Wood is a happy, fair, honest place. Do you agree to that?'

Victoria Stitch gulped and stared out at the crowd. She didn't know what to think. This was all happening too fast.

'Come on,' boomed Celestine. 'Take back what Lord Astrophel has stolen from you all these years.'

There was such a look of hope and desperation in Celestine's eyes that Victoria Stitch found herself cautiously nodding her head. Celestine reached up and put her hands either side of the crown that Victoria Stitch was already wearing. It was huge and beautiful—gunmetal black and frosted all over with diamond stars.

'I hereby crown you Queen Victoria Stitch of Wiskling Wood,' said Celestine, loudly and firmly. Unlike at her own coronation, where the crowd had erupted into cheers, there was an awed, shocked silence. Victoria Stitch forced herself to smile. Celestine beamed. A small breeze fluttered round the wood, making the trees rustle, and for a moment, the stars seemed to shine brighter. Celestine waved to the crowd, took Victoria Stitch's hand, and together they turned to go back inside the palace.

CHAPTER 28

AS soon as they were back inside, Victoria Stitch turned on Celestine.

'What was *that*?' she shouted, wiping at her eyes with her gloved hand. 'You made me look like a fool!'

Hurriedly, Celestine popped another of the sweets from the jar into her mouth to reverse the voice-magnifying spell.

'No!' she said. 'They saw your vulnerability. It was good!'

'It was embarrassing!' stormed Victoria Stitch. She ripped her crown off her head and threw it down.

'I can't be Queen of Wiskling Wood,' she said. 'I don't want to be!'

'But!' said Celestine, her face falling and tears

beginning to gather in her eyes. 'You have to be. I *need* you here! I thought this is what you always wanted?'

'I won't be made to do anything!' said Victoria Stitch. 'All you've done is make yourself less popular! I'm going back to Naomi!'

'No!' begged Celestine. 'Please! Stay with me. I need you. I can't raise the diamond baby on my own!'

Victoria Stitch stared at her twin.

'What?'

Celestine blinked, her eyes glittering with tears beneath her long wiskling lashes.

'There's a new diamond baby growing on the wall of the crystal cave,' she whispered.

Victoria Stitch didn't say anything, just stared at her sister. Celestine couldn't tell what she was thinking, but there was a faraway look in her eyes.

'You'll be a great mother, Celestine,' she said at last. 'But I can't stay. I just can't. I don't want to.'

Then she turned on her heel and marched out of the room.

Immediately two palace guards hurried after her.

'Where are you going . . . er, Your Majesty?' they said. 'Even the Queen is not permitted to leave the wood without an explorer's badge. You don't have the correct training.'

Victoria Stitch shrugged the guards off.

'I can do whatever I please!' she said primly.

'They're right,' said Celestine, hurrying after Victoria Stitch. 'You can't leave. No one's going to let you go unescorted from the palace now that you're queen.'

Victoria Stitch whirled back around to face Celestine. This time there was a dark expression clouding her face.

'Don't even *try* to trap me!' she warned. 'I won't be *trapped!*'

Suddenly something snapped inside Celestine.

'*You're* trapped?!' she cried. 'Do you know how stifled I've felt since becoming Queen—while you've been out in the human world, free to do whatever you like? I'm never allowed to go anywhere without being accompanied, I've been subtly being controlled by Lord Astrophel. You know nothing of what it feels like to be trapped!'

'You forget, I've been in prison,' said Victoria Stitch, laughing derisively and narrowing her eyes.

'You were in prison for *two days*!' shouted Celestine, starting to feel really angry now. 'And who helped get you out? Me! Since then you've been cavorting in the human world, doing whatever you please, not even considering the danger you might be putting us all in!'

'I did consider you,' hissed Victoria Stitch. 'I thought about you *all the time!*'

'Well then why are you always doing things to *hurt* me?' shouted Celestine. 'I never wanted to be Queen! You know that. But here I am, doing my duty. Lord Astrophel ripped us apart. But I've put us back together again and you're just rejecting it all!'

Victoria Stitch felt her insides twist into knots. She felt such a strong urge to go back to the human world, back to Naomi, and the place where she was adored. The memory of Celestine's speech made her cringe. She had *cried* in front of the crowd. They had seen her mask slip.

And now there was the diamond baby, too . . .

Victoria Stitch glanced at the palace guards standing either side of her. If she was going to leave, she'd have to do it sneakily.

'I'm going to bed,' she said. 'We can talk about this in the morning, Celestine.'

Then she stalked out of the room.

Celestine watched her sister go, knowing in her heart of hearts that Victoria Stitch would be gone by morning. Tears ran down her face, sparkling in the moonlight and landing on her shoes with little splashes. How could Victoria Stitch be so cold and cruel?

CHAPTER 29

IT was very early morning when Victoria Stitch arrived back at the cottage. She had used the sleeping spell with wild abandon to get back out of Wiskling Wood again—it wouldn't matter, she was never going to go back! Then she had flown, hunched down on her bloom, as fast as she could back to Naomi. She landed on one of the upstairs windowsills and peered in through a crack in the curtain. The light was on in Naomi's bedroom. She was already up! Victoria Stitch banged on the glass with her tiny fists, but Naomi didn't come. Huffing, she got back onto her bloom and flew round the side of the house where she slipped through the letterbox, tearing her dress as she did so. The house was dark and sleepy except for a light coming from the kitchen. Victoria Stitch flew towards it, pleased to see that both Naomi and Elizabeth were in there. Elizabeth was an early riser, anyway, but had Naomi waited up for her all night?

Naomi was busy sprinkling a large helping of marshmallows onto a swirl of whipped cream, deep in conversation with her mother. Victoria Stitch stopped just outside the doorframe. It sounded like they were having an important conversation.

'I'm sorry, my love,' Elizabeth was saying. 'It was wrong of me to not be more encouraging of your talents. I was just so scared of you not being secure when you're older but . . . you're right. You should be going to art school one day. I can see it now! You're brilliant!'

Naomi beamed up at her mum.

'You really think so?' she said.

'I know so!' said Elizabeth. 'And everyone else can see it, too. How many articles and magazines have Victoria Stitch's outfits been mentioned in?'

Naomi shrugged as though she didn't really care, but Victoria Stitch could see she was glowing.

'You have real talent, Naomi,' said Elizabeth. 'And you're only thirteen! I'm so proud of you.'

Elizabeth pulled Naomi into a huge hug and held her for a long time. Victoria Stitch found her throat closing up with emotion as she watched them both. Always on the outside looking in. A long-buried wish rose up within her and she tried to push it back down as she always did.

It *would* have been nice to have a mother.

Victoria Stitch tried to shake the unwelcome thought away. There was no point wondering about that sort of thing. It was too late for her to have a mother.

But . . . the thought nagged at her. Could she be that wiskling for someone else? Give it the things she wished she'd had?

Could she?

No! Of course, she couldn't. It was an absurd thought. She was too spiky. *Unlikeable!*

But . . .

Victoria Stitch shook the thought away.

'I feel so much better this morning!' she said, haughtily as she flew into the kitchen.

'Victoria Stitch!' cried Naomi, jumping up.

'That's good,' smiled Elizabeth. 'I must say, it's rare to see you two up so early!'

Victoria Stitch and Naomi glanced at each other.

'Well,' said Elizabeth. 'I must get ready for work. And, Naomi, you must get ready for school. And remember we're both going out to the cinema tonight. With Liam!'

Then she disappeared from the room, humming.

Naomi smiled.

'I like Liam,' she said. 'And he's good for Mum. She's so happy at the moment!'

'I'm glad,' said Victoria Stitch, and she landed on the counter, next to Naomi's giant mug of hot chocolate.

'So, tell me what happened!' said Naomi, leaning in close. 'I've barely slept a wink worrying about you. Why have you got all those blue stains on your tights?'

'It's just blood,' said Victoria Stitch.

'Blood!' said Naomi, shocked. 'What happened? Is Celestine OK?'

'She's . . . OK,' said Victoria Stitch, though inside she knew that wasn't true. Celestine wasn't OK at all.

She took a deep breath, feeling her heart break just a little.

'Naomi,' she said. 'I think I have to leave you. I don't want to but I have to. I need to go back to Wiskling Wood. I'm sorry.'

Tears sprang to Naomi's eyes.

'What?!' she said. But *why?*

'Celestine needs me,' said Victoria Stitch. 'I can't let her down again. I've let her down so many times. And there's another wiskling, too. I can't let them down, either.'

Naomi nodded. Sniffed.

'And I can't keep being a celebrity in the human world,' said Victoria Stitch. 'I know that now. It's putting Wiskling Wood at risk. It was wrong of me. I've been given another chance, Naomi. I need to take it. For Celestine's sake and for . . . the sake of the new diamond baby.'

'The new diamond baby?' asked Naomi, her eyes widening in shock. 'I remember you telling me about diamond babies. Does that mean . . . ?'

Victoria Stitch grinned.

Naomi gasped, and suddenly her sad expression changed to one of resoluteness.

'You *must* go back,' she said. 'A baby needs a family. I don't know what I'd do without Mum. And . . . well, I wish my dad was still here, but at least I had eleven years with him.'

A single tear rolled down her cheek, and Victoria Stitch wished she could wrap her arms around her best friend and give her a big hug.

Naomi sniffed again.

'It's the right thing to do,' she said.

'I know,' said Victoria Stitch, hanging her head. 'And aside from all of that, I can't leave Celestine on her own with a baby. She won't know what to do! We didn't have a mother.'

'Of course,' whispered Naomi. 'I'm going to miss you like crazy, though!'

'I'll miss you, too,' said Victoria Stitch. 'But I'll come back and visit you. As often as I can! I'll persuade them to give me an explorer's badge so I can leave the wood whenever I like,' she said gleefully.

'I would love that,' smiled Naomi, though her eyes were glittering with tears.

'What will I tell everyone? Lily? Mum? The museum?'

'I'll write them a letter,' said Victoria Stitch. 'You can give it to them.' She scrabbled in her bag for a pen and paper. Naomi leant close, marvelling at Victoria Stitch's minuscule handwriting.

Dear humans,

I have had a magnificent time here in your world. I have loved (nearly) every moment. But the time has come for me to go back to Fairyland. I am sorry to disappear like this, but Fairyland needs me. I am afraid I won't be back. Thank you for everything.

Love and glitter,

Victoria Stitch—Queen of Fairyland

P.s. Don't go looking for me, or you'll be cursed!

Victoria Stitch folded up the letter and handed it to Naomi.

'What about your money?' asked Naomi.

'You can have it,' said Victoria Stitch. 'Use it for art school. Maybe donate some to the museum. They spent a lot of money on my beautiful palace.'

'That's true,' said Naomi. 'I'll do that. Thank you Victoria Stitch. You've been SO wonderfully *magic!* Memories of our time together will inspire me for a lifetime! Being your friend has felt so special.'

'No!' burst out Victoria Stitch, suddenly. 'Thank *you,* Naomi! You built me back up when I was almost broken. If it weren't for you I'd be . . . I'd . . . I don't know what I'd be. But I'm glad I met you. You're my very best friend! I love you!'

'I love you, too,' said Naomi. 'I wish I could hug you!' She held out her little finger and Victoria Stitch squeezed it tightly, wrapping her arms right around it and pressing her cheek to Naomi's skin.

'I'd better go now,' she said after a few minutes. 'Before I change my mind!'

She let go of Naomi's finger and got back onto her bloom.

'Keep my doll's house safe for me, won't you?' she asked. 'With all its special things in it. I'll be back! To visit you sometime. In secret.'

'I'll keep it safe!' nodded Naomi, earnestly. 'I promise! It will be waiting for you.'

Victoria Stitch turned her face away as she got onto her bloom and rose up into the air. She found herself unable to say anything else without the words choking in her throat. She whizzed out into the hallway, and Naomi followed, opening the front door so that she could fly out in a flurry of twinkly sparks. Victoria Stitch waved sadly as she wheeled round in the air before shooting up towards the rising sun, into the pink sky, and back towards Wiskling Wood.

CHAPTER 30

A few hours later, Victoria Stitch stood outside Celestine's bedroom door.

'She's not up, yet,' Minoux had informed her when she had arrived back at the palace, silently promising herself that it would be absolutely the last time she would use any underhand spells from the *Book of Wiskling*.

'In bed?' said Victoria Stitch. 'But it's almost midday!'

'I know,' Minoux had whispered worriedly. 'And she's supposed to be doing a speech about the new diamond baby in a few hours' time!'

Victoria Stitch had crept up to her sister's room and now stood in front of it, feeling a stirring of anxiety in her chest. Gingerly she pushed open the door and peered in through the dim light. The curtains were drawn, but Victoria Stitch could just make out her sister, curled up in a tight ball in the middle of her bed.

'Celestine,' she whispered.

There was no response.

Victoria Stitch hurried over to the bed and climbed under the covers, shuffling up to Celestine's warm body, wrapping her arms around her.

'I'm sorry I ran away,' she whispered.

Celestine still didn't say anything, but her antennae flickered with gold sparks.

'I was scared,' said Victoria Stitch.

There was silence, and then . . .

'I'm scared, too,' said Celestine.

Victoria Stitch hugged her sister tighter.

'I'm here to stay,' she said. 'I promise.'

Celestine turned round to face Victoria Stitch.

'Really?' she asked.

'Yes,' said Victoria Stitch.

Celestine blinked, her eyes glassy.

'We never had a family, only each other,' she whispered.

'I know,' said Victoria Stitch. 'And so we're going to be the best family for this new diamond baby! I'll be like the fun aunt. You can be the mother!'

Celestine's mouth twitched into a smile.

'Why can't I be the fun aunt?'

'Because you're the one the baby will love most,' said Victoria Stitch. 'Obviously.'

'That's not true!!' said Celestine reaching out to hug Victoria Stitch back tightly. 'But Aunt Stitch does have quite a nice ring to it.'

CHAPTER 31

ELEVEN MONTHS LATER . . .

VICTORIA Stitch and Celestine flew high in the sky together on their blooms, flanked by four palace guards. Victoria Stitch was no longer using Celestine's old buttercup but had managed to find her old bloom—a beautiful, regal, hot-pink rose—from where it had been locked away by Lord Astrophel. It had been one of the first things she had done once she had returned to the wood, along with renovating a portion of the Great Oak Palace to suit her own Gothic tastes.

'I can't believe the day has come!' said Celestine, nervously, as they flew along in the direction of the

Crystal Cave.

Victoria Stitch was uncharacteristically nervous, too. She had never imagined being entirely responsible for another wiskling.

It hadn't been easy at first, being back in Wiskling Wood. She had felt unwelcome, like a stranger who shouldn't be there. But Celestine had worked hard to make her feel accepted and things were getting better. The outrage and fear wisklings had felt over Victoria Stitch's escapades in the human world were starting to fade, and the wood was getting used to having two queens. It had helped that there was a new diamond baby on the way. The newspapers and magazines were full of speculation about the impending prince or princess, the Buttonsponge Bakery released a new limited-edition cupcake, with glassy sugar diamonds sprinkled over the top, and the palace had been showered with beautiful gifts for the royal nursery.

'Look at this!' Celestine had said only that morning at breakfast, as she held up a tiny sleepsuit with flower-petal frills and pom-poms on the toes.

'I prefer these,' said Victoria Stitch, holding up a pair of tiny black booties studded all over with diamond stars.

Just then there was a knock on the door and a footman entered holding a golden envelope. Celestine

looked at Victoria Stitch and Victoria Stitch stared
back at Celestine in shock. A golden envelope! Could
it be *the* golden envelope? The one they had been
waiting for?

'It's from the Crystal Cave,' said the footman,
handing it to Celestine, and Victoria Stitch's heart
immediately began to beat fast. Celestine slit the
letter open with a fingernail and a cloud of twinkling
dust puffed out of the envelope as she slid the card out
from inside.

'What is it?' asked Victoria Stitch impatiently. 'Tell
me!'

'Our baby is here!' said Celestine, her cheeks flushed
pink. 'She cracked out of the diamond this morning
and she's ready for us to collect her!'

'She?' said Victoria Stitch.

'Yes!' said Celestine. 'It's a little princess!'

Now, Victoria Stitch and Celestine stood in front of the golden gate outside the Crystal Cave, at the base of Wiskling Mountain, waiting for the Crystal Keeper to open it.

'Your Majesties,' he said, twisting the key in the lock. The gate swung open and Victoria Stitch and Celestine stepped into the cave. Its walls glittered and twinkled all over with different coloured crystals—all holding tiny baby wisklings, growing inside.

'Where is she?' asked Victoria Stitch impatiently, tapping her foot. 'Show us!'

'*Please,*' added Celestine, shooting a disapproving glance at her sister. She was constantly having to remind Victoria Stitch not to be rude.

'If you can't say anything polite, just smile and nod,' she often suggested.

Victoria Stitch seemed to do a lot of smiling and nodding.

The Crystal Keeper led Victoria Stitch and Celestine to an office to the side of the cave. Inside it was a desk with a large official-looking book on it, an emerald-green velvet armchair, and a row of five small cot beds.

'She's here,' said the Crystal Keeper, hurrying over to one of the cot beds and lifting a tiny bundle from one of them. 'She's asleep.'

Victoria Stitch stared in awe, her breath catching in her throat as the Crystal Keeper held the baby out for her to take.

'You take her, Celestine,' said Victoria Stitch, standing back a little. Celestine took the baby and gazed down at it, her face breaking into an expression of wonder and delight.

The Crystal Keeper led Victoria Stitch and Celestine back out of the cave, where he left them standing by the twinkling brook that ran right past the entrance.

'It's been an honour, Your Majesties,' said the Crystal Keeper, bowing slightly before going back through the gate and locking it from the other side.

Celestine stopped looking at the baby for a moment to glance up and smile gratefully at the Crystal Keeper while Victoria Stitch stood a little way away, fidgeting. There was no one else around except the guards. The Crystal Cave was not a place for the public.

'Don't you want to hold her?' asked Celestine.

'In a minute,' said Victoria Stitch, fluttering her sooty eyelashes. 'I don't think I'd be very comfortable for a baby. My arms are quite bony you know.'

'But you haven't even looked at her properly yet!' said Celestine. 'Come and see her face. She's so sweet!'

'In a minute,' said Victoria Stitch again. 'Let's decide

her name. How about Chocolate Button? I think it's a sweet name.'

'What!?' Celestine stared at Victoria Stitch, aghast. 'We can't call her that!'

'Why not?' asked Victoria Stitch. 'I like unusual names. I like chocolate. And I like buttons.'

Celestine raised her eyebrows.

'How about Dezdemona?' suggested Victoria Stitch. 'Or Ethelbert? They're nice and Gothic.'

'She doesn't look like a Dezdemona,' said Celestine, rolling her eyes. 'Or an *Ethelbert!* You need to *look* at her before you give her a name.'

Before Victoria Stitch could protest again, Celestine walked over and placed the baby in her arms. Victoria Stitch looked down in horror at the tiny wiskling, who was still shimmering all over with jewel dust. And then her expression changed to one of utter wonderment. The baby was beautiful. She had a tuft of pale pink hair and skin that looked as soft as rose petals. Victoria Stitch felt her eyes prick with tears. This baby was all hers and Celestine's responsibility. She was so small. So fragile! It reminded Victoria Stitch of exactly how tiny and fragile she had felt compared to Naomi and all the other humans. How *miniature* she was.

'She reminds me of Minoux, with the pink hair,'

observed Celestine.

Minoux.

Miniature.

'Let's call her Minnie,' said Victoria Stitch, suddenly. 'Minnie Stitch.'

'Minnie Stitch,' said Celestine, smiling. 'Yes, I like it.'

She held out her arms to take Minnie back, but Victoria Stitch held on tightly.

'Not yet,' she said, turning away. As she did so, Minnie opened her eyes and gazed up at Victoria Stitch. Her little antennae flashed with tiny, diamond sparks. And then she smiled! Victoria Stitch beamed back, her own antennae glittering, like two silver sparklers. Suddenly she felt a sense of belonging like she never had before. She was in exactly the right place. Here in Wiskling Wood with her sister Celestine— and now with Minnie, too. Three diamond wisklings together. They both needed Minnie, and she needed them. They belonged together. They were a family.

Victoria Stitch beamed down at Minnie, her cherry-pink lips curving upwards into the biggest smile. A smile laced with love and mischief.

'Princess Minnie Stitch,' she whispered. 'Oh, the adventures we'll have! I'm going to teach you to be all kinds of bad and glittering!'

EPILOGUE

THREE YEARS LATER . . .

VICTORIA Stitch and Celestine sat together in the sitting room of the Great Oak Palace. Golden afternoon sunshine streamed in through the large, arched window, and outside the leaves rustled, glowing like emeralds in the light.

'Found it!' came a little voice from over the other side of the room, and Minnie came bounding across the carpet towards her mother and aunt, clutching a book triumphantly in her small fist. Celestine laughed.

'Did Aunt Stitch try to hide it again?' she asked.

Victoria Stitch didn't say anything but primly fluttered her eyelashes. Minnie bounced onto the sofa and snuggled down in between Victoria Stitch and Celestine.

'It's my favourite book,' she said.

'Humph,' said Victoria Stitch. 'It should never have

been allowed to be published! The ending is atrocious! And the author got so many details wrong!'

'Oh, it's just a bit of fun,' said Celestine. 'I think you secretly love having a book written about you. And it's a good warning tale for young wisklings against showing themselves to humans.'

'Read it, Aunt Stitch, read!' begged Minnie, waving the book so close to Victoria Stitch's face that it almost bopped her on the nose.

Victoria Stitch sighed and took the book, admiring the illustration of herself on the front cover. It *was* a flattering likeness.

'Well, alright Minnie,' she relented, putting her arm around the tiny pink-haired diamond princess. 'But *only* for you.'

Minnie gazed adoringly up at her aunt and her antennae fizzled with happy peachy pink sparks.

Victoria Stitch opened the book and began . . .

VICTORIA
STITCH

A warning tale for young wisklings
(never show yourself to a human)

By Winika Berry

Victoria Stitch loves being Queen.

Being Queen means she eats
diamonds for breakfast . . .

. . . and thinks she can break all the rules!

One rainy afternoon,
Victoria Stitch
felt bored.

She decided that it was time
that humans saw how
much she SPARKLED.

So she carefully
folded herself up
and climbed into
a black envelope.

It requires a
forbidden spell
to do this
and a
horribly

crooked

imagination.

The next morning, a human called Noomi
discovered a black wriggling envelope on the doormat.

From this envelope burst a tiny wiskling
in an explosion of glitter and perfume.

'You must be a fairy!' said Noomi.

'I am Victoria Stitch,
and I am the Fairy Queen!'
Victoria Stitch said.

'I am so very
beautiful! I am a
work of art!'

At first, Noomi
was pleased
to have a *fairy* in
her house.

But it wasn't long
before she discovered
that Victoria Stitch
was a *troublemaker*.

Victoria Stitch liked to take daily walks across Noomi's dressing table.

She liked to leave her mark.

Sometimes she stopped for a tea party
with Stardust, but Stardust didn't like tea,
so they ate raspberry ice cream instead.

Neither of them liked tidying up.

One morning, Noomi announced that she would be hosting an exhibition of her artwork in the gallery downstairs. Her most respectable art-loving friends would be attending.

There would be tea and cake and sophisticated conversation.

Victoria Stitch smiled wickedly. 'We must be good tonight,' she told Stardust, wagging her pointy finger at him.

When the guests arrived,
Victoria Stitch was
swinging
from the chandelier
and staring at everyone
with her big eyes.

Nobody noticed her until . . .

SPLOSH!

She fell right into Duke Cornelius
Crumpet's cup of coffee.

Victoria Stitch leapt out of the cup
and jumped onto the tea table.

She ran across the cloth, leaving nasty
brown coffee stains in her wake.

Baron Von Spiral tried to grab her, but
she bit his hand with her sharp teeth.

'How dare you try to catch a queen!'
shrieked Victoria Stitch.

She unwrapped a sweet and put the wrapper
about her shoulders like a shiny cloak.

Then she started to climb up
the tiered celebration cake . . .

. . . knocking off the cherries and
leaving footprints in the buttercream.

The guests were not impressed.
And neither was Noomi.

Victoria Stitch
stood on top
of the cake.

'This will be my throne!'
she announced, holding
the candle up in the air and
lighting it with her wand.

Then, slipping in the sticky icing,
she accidentally dropped the candle
into a starfruit trifle.

The trifle was laced with brandy.
It burst into flames.

Baron Von Spiral leapt away
as a spark caught onto his moustache.

Standing among the blazing puddings,
Victoria Stitch took off her cloak
and held it above her head.

The heat from the flames
lifted her into the air,
and she floated regally on
her sweet-wrapper parachute
back up to the chandelier.

With raised eyebrows and snooty noses,
the guests all left the party, and Noomi
was left with the desecrated dining table.

She plucked Victoria Stitch from the chandelier.

'Put me down! I am the Queen!'
shrieked Victoria Stitch,
gnashing her teeth.

'That's quite enough
of that,' said Noomi,
taking one of the
framed prints
off the wall.

She undid the back
and quickly slipped
Victoria Stitch
behind the glass.

Then she stood back to admire her handiwork.

·FOR SALE·

'There. Now you really *are* a work of art!'

The end

HARRIET MUNCASTER

HARRIET MUNCASTER is an internationally
bestselling and award-winning children's author
and illustrator. She spent her childhood drawing,
writing, and creating miniature worlds for tiny characters.

She lives near some beautiful hills in Bedfordshire,
England, with her husband and daughter.